Chester Gore Miller

Chihuahua

a new and original social drama in four acts

Chester Gore Miller

Chihuahua
a new and original social drama in four acts

ISBN/EAN: 9783337383503

Printed in Europe, USA, Canada, Australia, Japan

Cover: Foto ©Andreas Hilbeck / pixelio.de

More available books at **www.hansebooks.com**

CHIHUAHUA.

A NEW AND ORIGINAL SOCIAL DRAMA

IN FOUR ACTS.

BY

CHESTER GORE MILLER.

(Dramatic Work, the first:)

———

Without money, life is but existence, nothing more.

I would say that of him who can dissemble successfully, Nature has conferred a priceless gift.

I do not want my confidence in human nature strengthened, for tomorrow would only shatter it.

CHICAGO, ILL.
KEHM, FIETSCH & WILSON CO., PUBLISHERS
119 LAKE STREET.
1891.

CONTENTS.

PREFACE.

During the winter of 1884, in San Francisco, California; the author while reading Deluze's work on animal magnetism, first conceived the idea of using the subject as a plot basis. The play was outlined and laid away. Taken up and completed between the 9th and 23rd of December, 1889, in New York City; copyrighted in January, 1890, and revised at various times to the present form.

> It is true, that though much within
> Resembles much without; still
> I tried to look beyond the old; and not
> Intentionally borrowed from about.

THE AUTHOR.

DEDICATION.

To one of the dark agencies of life ;
I inscribe this epitome of much.

DRAMATIS PERSONAE.

Walter Emory, alias Mr. Sumner of Tombstone.

John Emory, alias Mr. Bowie of Chihuahua.

Jackson Fremont, broker on New York Mining Stock Exchange.

Lieut. Ray Silverton, U. S. Cavalry, Arizona.

Mr. West, Mr. Fremont's accountant.

Ex-Senator Choate, lawyer and notary.

Cicero, a butler.

Mrs. Fremont.

Hazel Emory, her daughter.

Lotta Prescott, cousin and ward of Mrs. Fremont.

Mrs. Kelton, mother of Mrs. Fremont.

Lady and gentlemen guests, in Act II.

SYNOPSIS OF SCENES.

PLACE—New York City.

TIME--The Present.

ACT I.—Private office of Mr. Fremont, Wall Street.— Afternoon.

ACT II.—Drawing room of the Fremont mansion, Fifth Ave.—That evening.

ACT III.—Conservatory—One month later.

ACT IV.—The Library—Two months later.

PROLOGUE.

In the perusal of this infliction,
Don't gauge it all as empty fiction;
But study close and you will find
Many ideas of a light and darkened kind,
To assert a shape, to design a lesson.
Take the character of Monte, not universal;
A direct contradiction of our Nation's motto,
E Pluribus Unum—Latin—"One of many."
This, on the golden and silvered face
Grace it, we do read it.
So in life's construction, these very words,
Three only, do we read you on
The darkened, the brighter and the many surface.
She is one of many, he is one of. many.
They the same; nations may be marked:
Whether for the innumerable multitude
Of situations attendant on this life
Of individuals, republics or empires.
In this prologue, this triumvirate of words
Is hampered with exceptions:
For exceptions do claim respect;
Speaking of one, only one of many a one;
And this, a singular person, will rise up
In truth to win an affirmation.
The name is genius, here the Latin stumbles;
Genius, which always remains one of few.
Sumner is in the vicinity;
A master of himself and others:
Intellectual, ambitious, passionate and cold,
His mind a practiced reasoner's sway does hold:
A general in the army of the narrow minds,
To deceive himself he is not so blind;
He bargains with success and pays the price.
Of the balance, there exist a multitude
Kindred to their dispositions:
Kindly let them go for what they are,
To brace the principal, not to mar.
Now leading man please do not swagger
When you characterize Mr. Sumner. Neither
Weary your audience with long speeches
And lengthy, tiresome discourse;
For much herein is writ to cut.

ACT I.

Scene—*Private office of Mr. Fremont, Wall St.*
Afternoon.

*Fremont—Standing at window looking out; raining
heavily; wind whistling.*

What depressing effect accompanies such weather;
Darkened skies; rain driving in torrents; wind
Whistling in mournful sighs down the chimney flues;
Telling to my imagination sorrowful tales;
Stories of phantoms; what chilling influences.
The hour is as an evening one, it is late:
Four o'clock; deserted streets; business about over.
It was a stormy day quite like this,
Nine years ago—that—but why recall the memory?
What—again! again!—another presentiment?
When some event
Unfortunate to our interests has happened, an occasion
Of by-gone years; some trifling incident or thought,
Bring back to the memory
From the shadows of the past a presentiment
Of the event or events to come. It seems
Like a grim vision of warning; it startles us;
Our power to resist its force is gone.
A dark foreboding, it leaves a deep impression;
To shadow our minds; make our rest a troubled dream;
Our waking moments a misty vision of the near future;
A nightmare of the day; snatches of real incidents;
Fanciful ghosts of idle thoughts;
A grand conglomeration of everything;

Like a great drama constructed of many ideas;
Such is its composition : and to the superstitious
Records an omen and means much;
To thinking and enlightened minds
Records but a phase of Nature's queer laws
And ways yet dark to philosophy, and means nothing.
Why will the past keep so attendant on me
To the exclusion of more weighty thoughts?
What need of this last serious stroke
Of this mental torturer?—unknown.
Why will the memory of this long years ago episode,
Seek companionship with the happier moods?
Casting a baleful shadow o'er my peace of mind.
Vague impressions have assailed me the past week.
Is this the punishment a man who happens once
To have done a piece of financial work,
In the light as hardly square, has to endure?
Am I weak?   most certainly so:
Yet if I reckon aright, those men history call brave
Have had their conscience pricked now and then
By sundry well-nigh forgotten scandals.
It goes by report that stock brokers
Have not a conscience, I must be an exception.
I will once more read over the letter
That rests foundation to these apprehensions.

Rings bell—Enter West.

Fremont. West, bring me the box numbered one,
On the third shelf to the left. *Exit West.*
Again will I attempt to ease a conscience
Too easily troubled by trifles; but then what a world
Of mournful sighs lies encompassed in those words.

Enter West, with dusty tin cash box.

West. Here is the box, but laying so long
Undisturbed by inquiring hands,
It is enveloped by dust and cobwebs
In a mantle of dull leaden color.

Fremont. Mind not the looks West; its color
Gives to it an air of well kept wisdom;
Of hoarded treasures of a long past period:
Should custom not to shortly change
Its burial mode, to consign us to the flames;
We'll rest under a fathom of the solid earth;
Relegated to the long slumbering peacefulness
Of an evolution from material life
To flaky dust. What are the latest reports?

West. Business dull, not much doing. Comstocks firm.
Oil weak.

Fremont. Any one in for me?

West. Only the Lieutenant; I said you were busy;
he wouldn't wait; said he might call later, as he desired
to see you in private.

Fremont. Call some one, call; Devil you may,
If you will but liven up this dull day.
Announce the next.

West. Very well.—*Exit.*

Fremont. What a history this little key unlocks. What
Unimagined mysteries some tin boxes contain.
Did their sides speak; what of importance
They could convey. In this city's social lists
Many a man rated high, would tremble;
Did that which find their refuge here,
Be opened to the broad light of public approval
Or condemnation, quite usually the latter.

Takes from box a letter.

An envelope, therein a letter;
Yellowing fast with the lapse of years:
It shows much handling.
'Tis not the first time I have read it:
A weakness to be acknowledged.
Why this subtle fascination?
There's little in it, nought but a threat.
Of no literary value;
A like excellence would place the writing.
But it's connected with a history,
A link in my life's eventful chain.
Thus is a letter, a relic, though nominal
In value: let it but have previous connection
With a past event of our lives,
It sometimes is given a two-fold reverence:
Be its cause for happy thoughts or sad ones.
Dated nine years ago,—*Starts*—
This very day!—

　　　　　　　　　　Tucson, Arizona, Nov. 20——
Jack Fremont:

For six months I looked for your return; you failed to
show up. The boy and I left for the North; the Apaches
got us; he was taken prisoner has undergone the usual
tortures and is at rest long before this. I escaped to
Tucson, heard later of your rise through "Epitaph Bill"
who bucked the tiger in York last winter. So the discoverer of the Chihuahua was left to die in the wilds of
the Southwest. You know my record as regards the old
troubles with others, I have still a notch to make.

　　　　　　My respects to your prosperity,
　　　　　　　　　　　　John Emory.

When last I saw him he counted his notches to a dozen. The report which spread abroad that he and his son died of fever in Sonora, still holds good; no word in nine years. Good lie well told, will a long time roll. He must be dead. His wife now my wife; I think he had his revenge when I married his wife; she is ambitious. Some people complain of having a skeleton in their lives; I feel at times as though I owned a graveyard. I am too weak; but then these mental strokes are frightfully realistic.—*Knock without.*—Come in.

Enter West.

West. A Mr. Sumner, asks to see you.
Fremont. His business?
West. Says private.
Fremont. Send him in.—*Exit West.*

Enter Sumner.

Sumner. Is this Mr. Fremont?
Fremont. The same.
Sumner. My name is Sumner; and I have a little business to transact that may require the limit of an hour. Would you kindly grant attention?
Fremont. The hour, Mr. Sumner, is yours; will you remove your coat?
Sumner. Gladly; bad weather out.
Fremont. Miserable; have a seat.
Sumner. Thanks. Now to my mission; it's the relating
Of a tale, that in justice to my delivery
You will drink in every word most thinkingly:
Though passing years mayhap have rusted some your
    memory,

As it is not a likely subject you'd keep polished up
In memory's storehouse, as for a ready interview.

Fremont.   Continue with the assurance I am an atten-
tive listener to what you may relate.

Sumner.   This dose may contain some bitterness;
But mark well my words to formulate reply,
And let your reason tarry on your answer.

Fremont.   Whatever be the import of your words
The bearing they carry will receive answer
Modelled to your text.

Sumner.   It's well.   Glancing backward fifteen years,
the exact date I do not recall; a Pacific Mail Steamer that
cleared from the port of Panama landed at San Francisco
one dark December day two men and a boy of nine
years——

Fremont. Nervously.   Yes, yes——

Sumner.   As a poet might say, Mr. Fremont;
Attune your ears to any new surprise, and
Let unbroken reel the thread of discourse
To an end.

Fremont.   Waves his hand to proceed.

Sumner.   They were strangers to the West; having left
New York six weeks previous; with two objects in view:
the father in search of health for the boy, the partner to
seek the golden fleece, and fleeced they were indeed.
Their names were John Emory, the father; Walter
Emory, the boy and Jack Fremont the partner.   You recognize the trio?

Fremont. Excitedly.   Yes, and I wish to hear no more;
what will you have?   What is your object in this?   And
with the greatest curiosity I would ask, who are you,
that you seem so well informed of this past?

Sumner. Has Nature so changed in nine long years of vicissitudes, hard and bitter fights with adverse circumstances, my countenance; that you fail to perceive some mark of recognition? Has your memory in these lapsed years so tarnished that you forget one so well known before? Walter Emory is the name by which I was formally known; and I am here to obtain what is lawfully mine.

Fremont. You lie! Becoming possessor to knowledge of a past episode of my career, you aim to hush a later day report. Walter Emory died by Apache torture in the State of Chihuahua, Old Mexico. I have the docu—— I have a memory and a good one. You are to me an adventurer! a——

Sumner. Make strong your accusations as you can; I know well just what I know, and barring further interruption I will continue.

Fremont. Silence I say! out of here quietly or I shall ring for an oficer.—*Rises.*—This blackmail shall not go on!

Sumner. *Seizes Fremont by the throat and hurls him into his chair, fixing upon him a piercing look the broker cannot meet.* Be resigned Fremont; keep your nerves more quietly employed than worried by opposing me. To resume, where left I off? O, where in selected language you failed to recognize me.

Fremont. *Aside.* I suppose I must hear it all, still he looks unlike the .boy.

Sumner. My mother and little sister remained in New York, my father intending to send for them as soon as he made a stake; but plans don't always pan out. Six years elapsed, the Eldorado still continued a vision of the obscure

future of the miner's luck. At last an outfit was made up
to prospect in Mexico, Chihuahua was reached; and
there in a far off and almost inaccessible canon in the
Sierra Madras the lode was struck. The bonanza was one
of the long lost Aztec mines of which the Indian romances
tell us. It was christened the "Chihuahua," to honor the
State that harbored it within its borders. Eureka! we
exclaimed; our troubles seemed to vanish; gold was in
sight. Ah, but how frail is the base of great expectations.
John Emory discovered the lode, Jack Fremont reaped the
benefit. Stand up temptation and a man, and the former
seldom falls. With a train of loaded mules, (they always
are,) each burdened with three hundred weight of high
grade ore, you left for Frisco to organize a company, float
the stock, to the manner of the day as now exists on Pine
Street and the Alley; return and work the mine and over
the hoisting works would read the legend "The
Chihuahua—Emory, Fremont & Co." The discoverer
and his son remained to guard the fortune found. The
company was formed; the stock was floated and disposed
of by you, not only your shares but those of Emory on
a boomed market, in the old reliable regulation way
memorial to Pine Street and the Alley. You neglected
to return; the deal collapsed; the company became a
myth; Fremont with the gained capital forgot its origin;
forgot his partner's friendship, a tie of years; which as a
rule in such cases holds good; a bond of love and fellow-
feeling made strong by the long struggle with poverty
and hardship; sundered it was: my father the rough and
unknown prospector, sunk in the wilds of a foreign
land—fortune's rattle—was dropped by his now wealthy
and former partner; six months travelled on; we left the

camp; a long journey; an Apache attack; I a prisoner to
eventually escape doomed thenceforth to wander homeless
and alone a child of fortune, now a man of a like occupation: my father was shot dead and left upon the field;
Fate hurled a parting gift upon him; he escaped the
Apache tortures. 'Tis not necessary for you to ask what
'tis I ask; no great financial gifts have yet been showered
upon me. My claim has all the sweetness of modesty
tinctured not by unreasonable requests; you are a million
aire, my share is half; too little by far in my philosophy
of the case; and but a short bit as the price of a father's life,
sacrificed by the duplicity of a trusted partner; a mother
and a sister of which I lost all trace though long have I
sought; the narrative's unreeled. Your answer?

    Fremont. Quite interesting a tale; who told it to you?
Your mind has talents more befitting an occupation
As a sensational novelist; then the lesser dignity
Of a fortune hunter, capitalled with vague wild tales
Of a romantic country, lost mines of the Montezumas;
Very amusing most enchanting yarn for so dull a day.
My child I am too old; take one more verdant
In financial fields than I, or try some one
More gullible than a broker of the regular board.
There's your answer, the door.

    Sumner. Locks door, puts key in pocket.
Mr. Fremont, favored terms must decide my future.
Alone in this great city; for New York
Is a hard place to be in, broke and friendless;
I would have suffered considerably,
Did not my valuable watch, in the action
Of a short remaining duty, *i. e.* till unwound,
Repose in mine uncle's safe; and

I swear I'll not hypothecate the ticket.
So——

Fremont. Damn you sir! leave this office, or I will
call for help!   I will——

Sumner. You will be silent.

Fremont. Now see here, my dear sir; my time is
precious, you are too important altogether, I can't listen to
such rot!

Sumner. As to my importance you can measure
Not too closely; as to your time
You value it beyond its actual worth
At present or in the near future. Your time to me
Is mine alone, of which I will profit as I use it:
For if I see aright, others will push well their affairs
With you; for this precious time might need to lapse;
An action time itself is not guilty of;
But rather of the being who chooses to consider
Time as his own. As to your title of the history,
It deserves a better appellation.

Fremont. You speak as if you would rule my destiny,
I am unused to dictation from a boy.

Sumner. One person is often the fate of another; for
in many ways the present controls the future and vice-
versa. True I look a boy that's because I shave. So
you'r a boy, as your reputation goes around the clubs.

Fremont. Sir! I——

Sumner. Shut up! To the charge of dictation; from
a dictator it is well to receive it with a bow; but from one
unused to mastery, the grounds are weak.

Fremont. This must stop right here, sir! Get out, or
I shall at the first opportunity give to the criminal court
an interesting case of a blackmailer wanting half my

fortune. Ridiculous! preposterous! Where are your proofs to this great claim? Go, draw your check on the United States Treasury; draft at the surplus; it's a larger fortune and you'd get it just as quick.

Sumner. For proofs, I have only the exact honesty of a related history you know too well. Have you a sheet of foolscap?

Fremont. Hands him paper. What next? going to draw your check? I beg of you one consideration, don't acknowledge me plotter in your furtherance of my suggestion.

Sumner. Tears off half sheet, folds in the shape of a cone. Yes, a most original check; a check to sarcasm, no longer am I to listen too. I shall not risk the law; you are wealthy; I penniless; though my cause has an honest claim for justice. Were I not schooled in that great virtue of policy I would shoot you down, for you murdered indirectly my father. In the courts my affidavit would read like a romance; no proofs to back it; for the contract made at the mine was verbal; consequently no damages: therefore I am compelled to be my own lawyer, judge and jury. Take of your mental freedom a brief farewell!— *Quickly draws vial, saturates cone with contents, springs on Fremont, grasps his throat, puts knee on chest, holds cone to nose.*

Fremont. Stop! What are you doing?

Sumner. Only applying this sickly fragrant perfume. The reason takes quick leave when chloroform has the call; what more potent drug exists when wanted for such a scheme? It was well I was prepared for the out-come. When he awakes his mastery will be but mild exertion.— *Smells cone, staggers back, catches at table, takes long breath.*—Too powerful!—*Throws cone in fire.*—Its effect may ruin the effect for which I used it.—*Shakes Fremont; no response; draws another bottle from pocket, and applies to nostrils.*—Ammonia will revive him.—*Fremont shows signs of reviving; Sumner draws chair before him; with eyes fixed on Fremont, and with hand proceeds to mesmerise him.*

Now to call into action that power
So priceless, so terrible. My magic fingertips,
Fail me not on your sleep producing mission.
O, most wonderful fascination of the mysterious,
Stay the throbbing pulse; lull to rest
The ceaseless workings of that cowardly brain;
And bring unto my orders the talents of its mind.
Bring subject to my will, his will;
So it would be a fallacy to state his will exists;
For it shall soon cease to call that frame
Its slave, if it ever has;
And must own to me I am the master mind.
Yes with slow but steady progression
That mind is being tranced; that soul
Which but a moment past, fired up at my words,
Is becoming dead; to replace itself within
Its palace, a more weakened king;
When 'tis my pleasure to release it
From the bondage of my commands.
O body of Fremont; when you arise
It will not be by the wishes of your will:
Though you will speak and act,
It will not be Fremont; not you alone
Who enacts the coming drama; only half:
Your brain's to let; I take possession;

And for its rental you will claim naught from me.
How sweet is power to rule the average mind!
These symbols of mediocrity to enslave;
To call their home my home:
No you'r not the first that's honored me
With a lease of their fast decaying faculties,
And has given to me this occult mastery of a soul.
I have not lived in vain, studied, worked and thought
For naught; but at this age though young,
Possess a wisdom of existing things,
Aged sage alone has right to call his own.
Had not your spirits been weakened
By fearful thoughts and weird weather;
My task to claim your soul, even with the aid
Of chloroform, would have been more extended.— *Wind.*
Thanks to your influence, rain, hail and sighing winds;
You are my fellow conspirators in this somber tragedy
Yet to be enacted; to right a long past crime.
    Sumner. Applies various tests to show complete control.
The absence of the will is proven,
No more his master; Fremont and yet not:
Fremont in body; Sumner in mind.
By my authority his mind is blank;
A lamentable reflection on its strength.
According to previous reconnoiterings,
His lawyer's name is Choate; his bookeeper West;
Including many minor informations gleaned,
That may partially light the way to a proper
Consummation of this unusual circumstance.
    *Knock without. Sumner gives key to Fremont, who
now completely under control acts and speaks as Sumner
directs. Sumner steps behind screen. Fremont opens door.*

Enter Lieutenant.

Lieut. Good afternoon, Mr. Fremont.

Fremont. How do.

Lieut. Bad weather to be abroad. This is my third call upon you today, but my object is such as inspires me to defy the maddest storm that ever wet a traveller. I wish your decision on a most important matter.

Sumner. Aside. Silverton!

Fremont. You are welcome. It's a gloomy day and my disposition is in sympathy with the time. But what am I to decide on?

Lieut. Mr. Fremont, to come to the point at once; a virtue soldiers should try to cultivate: I love your daughter and she loves me; I ask your sanction to our marriage. I possess no fortune but my good name; my family connections are honorable; my salary is the limit of my financial resources: but it is sufficient for two to live in a social way that would be modestly desirable. My hopes are many; and should the War Department consider favorably my recommendations, you will address me captain within a month.

Sumner. Aside. So I am destined to direct the marital aspirations of my friend, the Lieutenant, and once again today usurp Fate's occupation.

Fremont. Lieutenant, my determination regarding my daughter's hand would have but little weight. For I fear my lease of life is fast drawing to a close. You have my consent with all the best wishes of a father; but do not take this as a final answer; seek Mrs. Fremont, and to her make known the desires of your heart; for ere long she will be sole mistress of a part, of what of me financially remains.

Lieut. Thanks! you have my sincere thanks, for your consent. But your words are strange. You surely give no thought to death at your age?

Fremont. I do give death a thought; too many thoughts. Can you tell me where I will be just an hour from now? No. In this visit here be useful to two ends. Will you witness my will?

Lieut. Why certainly.

Fremont. I shall draw it up now.—*Rings bell.*

Enter West.

Fremont. West, send the boy for Choate; have him bring his seal; the business is important: and West, just cash this check.—*Writes check.*—Bring me the proceeds of its face.

Exit West.

Lieut. It's not bad policy to prepare the welfare of your friends; to die intestate can be most complicating to the lawful heirs. The making of a will, is a duty every business man should be cognizant of.

Fremont. Yes, it's a wise precedent. I want no quarrels over my property. The honored name of the house of Fremont, must be preserved. There's an ambition I have laid the greatest stress upon. In all my dealings in a business where much is charged as shady, I can look back on my record as being as square as the best of them; though the favored terms in which I speak are of myself.—*Knock without.*—Come in.

Enter West.

West. Announces. Senator Choate.—*Enter Choate.*— Here is the money.—*Fremont takes bills and puts in pocket.*

Fremont. Senator, how are you?

Choate. As usual. Yourself?

Fremont. Same. West, will you act as witness to my will?

West. Yes sir.

Choate. Ah, Lieutenant! am pleased to see you. Fremont, if you say same, you don't look same: you'r pale.

Fremont. So, well then the truth is I don't feel very active and a duty I've considered is the making of my will. I shall draw it up at once. You can attest and keep possession of the document. These gentlemen will witness for it. Its provisions I care to have known only to myself.

Choate. Proceed, friend Fremont, I am at your service. You will now perform a justice that heirs necessarily require from every moneyed man.

Fremont, *Writes at table. Choate, West and Lieut. withdraw to (L.)*

Choate. Lieutenant, you no doubt attend Mrs. Fremont's reception this evening? I wager there will be an attraction there you'd not forego for all the honors of the service.

Lieut. Yes, I attend. There's one who draws me by the witchery of her eyes; the gentleness of her voice; the beauty of her face; the delightful companionship one always finds with a lovely woman. For one who has had for the last fourteen months, only the dreary expanse of an Arizona desert, for the face of beauty; the hoarse exclamations of frontier companions for the gentleness of a voice; and the companionship of rough soldiers and cowboys, for the charm of ladies' society; he is soon taught to value the length of a leave of absence.

Choate. Lieutenant, you are young and susceptible; so West? The enchantment of a social existence is made stronger to one used to it, and yet deprived of its pleasures. When you are old as West or I, the gloss of silver, sheens your now dark locks; you may look with happy recollections perhaps with a cynic's smile at the memories of your younger years.

West. Just so; profound wisdom opens up to our minds as the years roll on; that is to the thoughtful man. And it is a phenomenal contrast between the actions of youth and the criticisms that age places upon them. For me, give me more age with the benefits time will bring.

Lieut. Announce not to me what the future may say, I care not, I live not, except for today.
To learn is to suffer——

Fremont. Gentlemen the instrument is finished;
It is brief, but you know—
The briefer be the considerations,
The less there are of cumbersome litigations.
Attest Senator.

Choate. Lieutenant, your name and address here.—
Lieut. signs.—Raise your right hand. Do you acknowledge this to be your own signature?

Lieut. I do.

Choate. Mr. West.—*West signs and raises hand.*—This signature, you acknowledge to be your own?

West. I do.

Choate. Affixes signature and seal.

Fremont. Seals will in envelope and writes, reads.—
"The last will and testament of Jackson Fremont. Not to be opened and read until two months from date of my death. Signed, Jackson Fremont."—*Gives envelope to Choate*

Choate. .Time yet to deposit it before the vaults are closed.. So I will leave you, to meet again this evening, when I hope to find you more at ease.

Fremont. Yes gentlemen, be on hand, we'll make the night hours merry. Good afternoon.

Choate and Lieut. Good day.—*Exit.*

West. Any further business to receive attention?

Fremont. Nothing I think of now.

West. Then I'll make for home; good night.

Fremont. Good night.—*Exit West.—Fremont sinks back into chair, motionless. Sumner comes from retreat; locks door; looks at Fremont and points to table—Fremont takes roll of bills from pocket and lays on table—Sumner takes bills—Fremont sinks back into chair.*

Sumner. That comes in conveniently. Interested Uncle give to me my watch. Five thousand dollars. What power has money to ease the rugged path and make light ones many troubles. Without money life is but existence nothing more. What danger poverty can generate. I can better seek my mother and sister now. Silverton said he was going to take me to a reception; didn't say where: no doubt the one Choate spoke of; Mrs. Fremont's Reception; possibly Fremont's wife! must be! then if so it's a most opportune chance for me. T'would be a selfish stab at fortune to ask for fairer luck. Fremont though not in the usual way you'll prance tonight.
O senseless form before me, man unmaned;
Convey to me, and an enlightened world,
Some unknown wonders.
Act to me something destined for a futurity;
Of this awful, this nighted science.
Make to me, by me and for me, as has been held,

A representative state in a legitimate way.
Arise when I enjoin, and issue forth
The silver flow of language,
Alike to Demosthenes or Cicero.
With hand of unnatural nerve, untutored
By proper guidance; write me
A Macbeth, a Hamlet or King Lear;
And blight the name of Shakespeare
With a more glorious fame.
Touch the violin and by the act
Gift Paganini to the present generation.   Write
Rhythmical lines, kin to Byron and to Burns,
To Longfellow, Bryant or to Gray.
Can I cause you; poor vacated head,
Moved by——and I, to sway the multitudes
By command: and let you grace or better still
Deface a Napoleon's throne,
And I the power behind it?
Man of two brains, what is your limit?
O, what are the possibilities of this age?

   *Gets coat and hat, looks at Fremont a moment, motions
with hand and says*—Awake.—*Quickly withdraws from
the room.*

   *Fremont.   Slowly awakes; appears dazed; stretches,
looks about, suddenly springs up with a shriek.*—What!
alone?   What does it mean?   Where have I been?   Have
I not just been conversing with a man who calls himself
John Emory's son?   Did he not seize me by the throat
and attempt to strangle me?— *Goes to glass.*—No marks!—
Sees tin box.—Now I recollect! I recollect! I was examin-
ing the box.   Yet I cannot be wrong, some one has been
here! West! I say, West!—*Goes to door and looks out.*—

He has left for home. Six o'clock! one hour past my
usual closing. He should have told me he was going to
leave; he always does. No doubt he did not wish to
disturb me.

Could it have been a dream?

Yes, only such: and yet why when Morpheus
Visits me in the drowsy afternoon hours,
Must great visions of damnable scenes
Go floating through my mind?
A phantasmagoria of fantastic thoughts;
That take the place of sweeter dreams.
O, Hell, thy bodily tortures damned,
Must be mild indeed, in comparison
To this mental misery!—*Sees letter.*—You again!
Why have I kept you to this late date,
To fret with your fast aging threats?
This is the end, no more: when you are gone,
Consumed in flames; my mind
In more exact and peaceful channels,
May hold its way.—*Throws letter in fire.*
Burn you cause of folly to a fool,
And in ashes lose the last record
Of a disagreeable epoch writ of my life;
That I preserved for use in court.
Now to dine at the club, then for home:
May the mirth of the coming night's enjoyment
Scatter seeds for happier thoughts
Throughout my early morning dreams.

END OF ACT I.

ACT II.

Fremont. Home: a sweet place to call my own;
To find rest in after running such a gauntlet
Of storms; the true harbor;
A haven many possess; many more seek;
And the majority are never fortunate enough
To call their own. Some without homes
Have many tribulations; others blessed
With homes, are often troubled quite as much.
I rank with the latter.

Enter Mrs. Fremont.

Mrs. Fremont. Jackson, how late you are! it is eight;
I had quite brought myself to the conclusion
You had deserted us for the club.
You look weary, haggard, pale; has anything
Happened to discord the day with you?
Fremont. Yes—no—yet not exactly so.
I cannot explain; my brain's bewildered.
My thoughts cannot call to themselves
The usual path of daily existence.
Today—this afternoon—late; I, alone
Within my private office, did have happen
A most mysterious—well I know not what
To call it; I may say with equal truth
A phantom or a reality:
So swiftly did the impression come and go.

T'was no less than that long dead son of yours,
Emory's boy, entered and announced himself;
Threatened me with vengeance for his father's death
As though it was I, that killed him—claim half
My fortune, yours and Hazel's inheritance.

 Mrs. Fremont. Emory! Emory's child, Walter! is he
  alive?   .
At this late date has he returnea, and vindictive?
Did he ask for me? Are you positive you saw him?
What did you do? What did you say?

 Fremont. Be not so rapid in your queries: that it was he
I have no doubt. But that he was there,
That he did speak to me, and threaten me,
Is not in my power to state. There lies
The mystification. That he attempted to strangle me,
Seemed to me evident: yet when I awoke
If it was an awakening; the light of the room
Was fast darkening into night's shadows;
I was alone. Everything lay undisturbed;
I called to West, he had left for home.

 Mrs. Fremont. Jackson, you shame me for you, that a
  dream
Should unnerve you so: you affect too much
That unwise past; stop it, see to your diet.
This report is a travesty on your sanity.

 Fremont. So I should judge, a dream; but what you
Call it, does not make it. I found no marks
Upon my throat; but for all this bleak afternoon
It has seemed to me, reason,
Cool and deliberate left the boundaries of my soul;
Sentiment took its place;
And I became as one hypnotized, helpless,

Swayed and bent as reeds in a storm;
The servant of those powerful weakening passions,
That go to make up the minds of men.

Mrs. Fremont. Fremont are you losing your mind?
You act as terrified as a child in the dark.
Come, go dress, liven up.
Cast away that fretful and haunted look,
As if you saw the ghost of death walking
By your side. You act strange of late;
Mumbling along, with bent head and corrugated brow
Quite like a man of ninety years.
Your thoughts are not to be valued to the price
Of their exertion. Leave now be quick.
Here arrive the first guests.

*Fremont. Hands behind back, walking as in deep
thought.*—I do not know. I cannot understand.—*Exit.*

Enter Sumner and Lieut.

Mrs. Fremont. Good evening, Lieutenant, you honor
us as the first to receive your hostess' greeting.

Lieut. Rather honor to myself, Mrs. Fremont. Allow
me, my old time friend and companion, Mr. Sumner.

Mrs. Fremont. I am delighted to meet you Mr.
Sumner. You are cordially welcome to our festivities.

Sumner. My happiness to be so welcome, Mrs. Fremont, is most sincere.

Lieut. Yes, Mr. Sumner is quite a stranger in New
York; but recently arrived from Tombstone, the famous
Arizona mining center.

Mrs. Fremont. I should judge social life in that far-
away spot would be found wanting.

Enter Hazel.

Mrs. Fremont. My daughter, Miss Hazel Emory, Mr. Sumner.

Sumner. Miss Emory, I am happy to meet you.

Hazel. Mr. Sumner.

Sumner. Aside. Emory! that is a strange coincidence. Hazel Emory.

Lieut. Takes Hazel's dancing card and writes.

Mrs. Fremont. Now with your indulgence, I shall leave you to yourselves a moment, so many require a hostess' attention.—*Exit.*

Lieut. There I am fortified against the rush.

Hazel. Lieutenant, how prompt you are; excepting the Senator you are the first to note a name.

Sumner. Ah, Miss Emory, am I not to be almost as prompt?

Hazel. Certainly, Mr. Sumner.—*Hands card to Sumner.*

Sumner. Starts to write, glances curiously at the Lieut.—Aside.—Ten dances.— *To Lieut.*—Lieutenant, you are prompt indeed; had I the fortune to be quite as such, I'd value much my bearing with the ladies' thoughts. Miss Emory, I'll mark for two; the Moonlight Waltz and the Bohemian Square. Thanks.

Enter Mrs. Fremont.

Mrs. Fremont. Now permit me, Mr. Sumner, to take you with me, and make you at home with the other guests.

Sumner. Charmed I'd be; with your permission, Miss Emory, Lieutenant.

Lieut. Go, and let me warrant you will never want a better guide, a more perfect hostess.

Sumner. Your estimate could not err in that.

Exit Mrs. Fremont and Sumner.

Hazel. Now Ray, what kept you? I expected you today. Forgot me did you not?   •

Lieut. Forgot you darling, t'would be better said to say I missed I lived, so much more applicable to such a charge. I did my best to gain the freedom of the afternoon, to make a companion to your sweet company; but I ran, and ran, and ran, only to find him at the last.

Hazel. Found, whom? Who could have kept my love on such a fruitless chase?

Lieut. It was not a fruitless chase, and yet it was in a measure of the word; your father was the object of my many journeys.

Hazel. Papa! what could you want with him? so urged by such anxiety.

Lieut. I shall let you guess the secret of this afternoon.

Hazel. Now Ray, did you? O what did he say?

Lieut. Told me to ask your mother; and if I am to have another such a chase, I'll take you and run off and let consent wait upon me after the knot is tied.

Hazel. Never mind, dear, such a duty is one sweetness of courtship.

Lieut. Yes love, an uncertain sweetness; a sweet bordered with a bitter, which might mix and gain for me no happiness only desperate resolution. Hazel dear, though your father denied not his consent, I fear your mother will oppose us; financial reasons you know. Though not suspecting our love, she will soon reason or condemn the fact, when hearing of the future possibility. Your father will mention it to her.   •

Hazel. Don't worry Ray, I shall make it all right with Mama.

Lieut. Yes, in my opinion if all the young ladies could make it right with Mama, what a world of gloomy reflections, some young·men might be saved.

Hazel. Quite true. Can Mr. Sumner dance? I see he is down for that dreadful Bohemian, in which the figures are so hard to remember; suppose he could not, just imagine the result of an attempt; I don't believe he can, Mama said after you left, that you said he was from Arizona.

Lieut. Now my darling, don't I dance? and I am from Arizona. I have never seen Monte dance, but I will wager a month's salary he is more proficient in that line than I. If he has seen as much dancing with the Spanish Senoritas as I have——

Hazel. Ray! Spanish girls, you——

Lieut. Have seen the boys at the Post do, he will not fail you this evening.

Hazel. I hope not. Isn't he handsome? such sparkling black eyes, they seem to look into your very soul, to read one's thoughts. He is coming now.

Enter Sumner.

Sumner. Pardon, have I interrupted?
Hazel. Not at all.

Enter Choate.

Choate. Found you at last, Miss Emory? Our dance is it not?

Hazel. So it is, Senator; excuse me, gentlemen.

Exit Hazel and Choate.

Lieut. Well Monte, has our charming hostess made the passing moments pleasant? Any hearts seeking hope? I swear those black eyes were made for other things than mere guidance of the way.

Sumner. I will flatter myself, my visit has not been in vain. Do you know Miss Prescott is a very charming girl, a beauty—

Lieut. Come now, don't lose your heart; give the others a chance.

Sumner. Now old fellow, take a little of that home,— ten dances,—ha! ha! My heart was crushed years ago, its passion for affection was blighted; had I one I'd not wait to give the others a chance.

Lieut. Yes I know they are always so; but a little more of Miss Prescott's company will make you another.

Sumner. Possibly. In my introduction to Mrs. Fremont, it seemed to me I had seen her face before, at some time or place in past years.

Lieut. Quien sabe. She was a widow when Fremont married her. Miss Emory is her daughter by her first husband. Emory was a mining man and died of fever in Mexico, years ago.

Sumner. Quite a history.—*Aside.— Very Coolly.—* I had hardly expected to find the man who ruined my father, had married my mother, and I a guest at her reception tonight; that Hazel Emory is my sister.

Lieut. You are thoughtful.

Sumner. Only a reverie. A thought of the past. I had once a very dear friend by the name of Fremont, who did me a service I shall never be able to repay; I was

wondering if our host could be the man. Such strange
coincidences do happen. I've not met him yet.

Lieut. There stands Mr. Fremont now, conversing
with Mrs. Madison.

Sumner. It is he! wonderful! I have fallen amongst
old friends.

Lieut. Congratulations extended. Your path to Miss
Prescott's heart is strewn with roses. Here, I must go, my
dance the next.—*Exit.*

Sumner. So my mother is my hostess;
Unknown to her the lost's returned.
My sister Hazel, that young lady; and I
Unknowingly consented to her marriage.
As for Ray, I'd ask to see no better groom.
Fremont my stepfather; thanks Fate
For your kind selection.
Of such a lovely sister, queenly mother,
Kindly grandmother I should be proud.
There can be policy in pride: spare Fremont,
And to-morrow I'd be escorted to the Tombs;
I'd lose my grip within a day;
Discovery would not be long delayed;
Choate would talk to Fremont, if not already.
It is a peculiar situation, and must receive
Immediate attention. The end may possibly
Fulfill the meaning occasioning the act.
O, not alone the sins but the misfortunes
Of the father are visited upon the children:
And often to retrieve the fault, genius and
Conspiracy will go to risky ends to gain
A beginning; and those ends are seldom known.
Now!—

Enter Fremont (R). Head bowed in thought, seats himself (L), does not see Sumner; Sumner glides behind chair, and begins silent manipulations; Fremont falls asleep; Sumner points (R); Fremont walks there and stops, with back to table; Sumner places small vial on table in (C) and walks to (L) looking sidewise at Fremont, who goes slowly to table, takes vial and exits (C).

Sumner. Within the seclusion of his room he will
Rest, till such time happens this evening
To place a desired opportunity within
My administration. It's a wise child
That can manage his stepfather.

Enter Lieut. and Lotta, Choate and Hazel.—Cicero crosses back of stage as others enter.

Hazel. Cicero, let me know when the Moonlight Waltz is called.

Cicero. Yes, Missa Hazel.—*Exit.*

Sumner. Come, disciples of Terpsichore, how is the evening passing?

Hazel. Delightful, I assure you. Have you met my cousin, Mr. Sumner?

Sumner. Thanks to the attention of Mrs. Fremont, my acquaintance with Miss Prescott, has dated from the early evening. I had the honor of the first dance, and it was very enjoyable.

Lotta. Quite so indeed.

Lieut. But where have you kept hidden? the ladies have noted your absence.

Sumner. Did the ladies miss me as I have often missed them, they would be forlorn indeed. My time has been

the property of your father, Miss Emory. In him, thanks
to Lieutenant Silverton, I have discovered a friend of long
years ago.

Hazel. How romantic, an old friend of Papa's!

Lotta. Do tell us about it!

Sumner. I will cry pardon! Let the recital await a
more convenient place and time, for the tale is long and
speaks of a generous act, few men are capable of: the
service Mr. Fremont rendered me.

Enter Cicero.

Cicero. Ladies and gemmens de conductah done am
call de Moonlight waltz.—*Exit.*

Sumner. Ours now, Miss Emory.—*To Lieut. and*
Lotta.—We will leave you to pleasant conversation or
follow in our wake as pleases you best.—*Exit.*

Lieut. Shall we dance, or have a quiet chat?

Lotta. I am a trifle tired, I would rather talk for a
change.

Lieut. You are of my thinking.

Lotta. Tell me, will you not feel just a jealous pang,
just a little uncomfortable, to have so handsome a man
with one you'll not deny you love?

Lieut. Non-troubling fancies: suspect Monte, so
square a friend, of trifling with the affections of one I
love; to believe he would seek to break the bond that
exists between us? No, Miss Prescott; Mr. Sumner is not
a friend of doubtful tendency. He is one of Nature's
noblemen; an honest generous man; a man of the world;
one who by force of circumstances has had to suffer and
endure: he has passed through great trials, though I know
little of his history.

Lotta. Is he not cynical? I remarked what appeared such expression flit across his countenance, once this evening; when he spoke of friendship and the value he placed upon it.

Lieut. Men who have experienced the ups and downs of life, are to a degree the servant of unfeeling thoughts. Yet I have known when times were the hardest his levity was greatest.

Lotta. Has he parents living?

Lieut. I understand he has no near relatives.

Lotta. How sad, and he has had to fight life's battle alone?

Lieut. Yes and won, for he is quite wealthy; speculates in mines; has an interest in many Mexican lodes.

Lotta. Then he is fortunate; his occupation is much in keeping with his dignity.

Lieut. By the way, I believe you said he was handsome?

Lotta. Why yes, don't you think so?

Lieut. He has a like opinion.

Lotta. Of himself? did he ever say—

Lieut. No, of you.

Lotta. You don't mean—did he really--

Lieut. Just what I said. Here comes Grandma.

Enter Mrs. Kelton. •

Mrs. Kelton. Enjoying yourselves, children?

Lotta. Yes indeed, Grandma; but did I not see you dancing the minuet with Mr. Powers? how could you be so giddy?

Mrs. Kelton. O dear me, and why not, pray? I as well as you? I am spry yet, my dear, if it was sixty odd years ago I danced the minuet at Andrew Jackson's Inauguration

Ball. Yes, dear, though I am close on to eighty years, I can still do my part when called upon by such a courtly gentleman of the old school, as Mr. Obadiah Powers.

Lieut. If we, Miss Prescott, fifty or sixty years hence can do as much, it will show the sophistry of the pessimists who entertain notions of the decay of longevity in the present state of society.

Mrs. Kelton. You are right, Lieutenant; we then lived just as high and had quite as many luxuries as you folks of this later generation, yet we lived, and you will do as well.

Enter Mrs. Fremont and Sumner.

Mrs. Fremont. Mother, resting from the dance?

Mrs. Kelton. Yes, daughter, I enjoyed it exceedingly; it took me back just sixty years.

Sumner. And let me add, I did not see more happy grace and perfect motion mid all the beauty of the room, then Mrs. Kelton did add to the minuet.

Mrs. Kelton. Then we all are happy.

Sumner. Now, Miss Prescott, the next is ours, allow me, my arm.

Lotta. With pleasure.

Sumner. With your permission, ladies, Lieutenant?

Exit Sumner and Lotta.

Lieut. My partner too, needs be found; is now awaiting me.—*Exit.*

Mrs. Fremont. This young man seems to carry well his part; of most agreeable manners for one whose life has been spent on the frontier.

Mrs. Kelton. There can be gentlemen on the border.
I believe I've seen, that face before, but where?

Mrs. Fremont. So to me, his features make mention
to my mind, of one at some time met; yet meeting so
many, don't tend to good memory. He is the gentleman
Lieutenant Silverton, asked me yesterday if I would
introduce to our circle; he's reported rich.

Mrs. Kelton. Where is Jackson? I have not seen him
on the floor to-night; many have asked for him.

Mrs. Fremont. Don't speak of him, he's lost his nerve,
and yet says he is a man. He returned from the office
frightened by a dream; I believe the man is losing his
mind. He walks the floor at night for hours; most trying recreation to my nerves: talks in his sleep; complains
of specters and fears, that make his peace a fight for
more quiet thoughts.

Mrs. Kelton. What is the cause?

Mrs. Fremont. O that old trouble; he fears
A mysterious vengeance of that husband of mine,
That died years ago. He robbed Emory
Of his rightful share, as you well know.
That's a past to which no remedy can apply;
A private history to be lost.
I loved Emory; if love is liking lightly;
But what gave he to me in ten years
Of married life? The troubles of a humble wife
Of a still more humble husband. Fremont made me
Socially. What is life to live as I then lived? So lowly,
So unknown, and I ambitious. If Fremont
Was smart enough to get the money and keep it,
'Twas his fortune: You know my determination,
Hazel or Lotta shall never marry but for gold.

I've experienced too much of genteel poverty
To sink them into loving arms, backed
By empty purses. I've no respect for the man
That is a man; and does not make his way.
How he makes it, I'd not inquire into;
So he makes it and keeps it.
A man of any brains has no business to be poor.
Many a great fortune has dark shadows over it:
But the possessors should keep it darker.
I tell you Jackson is weak; he is one of those
Who has done an unprincipled act, and when
Long past, must shudder o'er the remembrance.
The date is late to mend the past
I would not, could I.
Emory and the boy are dead, forget them.

Mrs. Kelton. Come, don't excite yourself or you will have a return of your spells. My opinions differ but it is not for me to argue dead issues of the Fremont family; you had better find Jackson and cause him to appear, his absence is noticeable.

Mrs. Fremont. He is no doubt in the smoking room.

Mrs. Kelton. I will go into the library to rest and think. Such a multitude of memories you have brought about.—*Exit.*

Enter Choate.

Choate. My entertainment is in your care this evening, and permit me to say, I am having a delightful time.

Mrs. Fremont. You look your words, Senator, and I am pleased; the evening is a great success.

Choate. But I have not seen Mr. Fremont, to-night, where can he have kept himself?

Mrs. Fremont. I saw him in the hall a short time ago, he complained of not feeling well.

Choate. What! no better? I wished him jollier wits for the evening.

Mrs. Fremont. You have met him to-day?

Choate. Was at his office late this afternoon, on an important errand, to attest his will.

Mrs. Fremont. His will! he said nothing to me about it. He was always very superstitious regards the making of such a document until the last moment. I often had thought he would die intestate. He is becoming quite thoughtful of the future.

Choate. Strange he did not mention it.

Mrs. Fremont. Yet hardly so. I have been so busy with the preparations for the evening, he no doubt thought best to wait till quieter hours to tell me of it. What were its provisions?

Choate. That I do not know. He desired the bequests to be known to himself alone.

Mrs. Fremont. Who witnessed for it?

Choate. Lieutenant Silverton and Mr. West. The will is not to be read until two months from the date of his death.

Mrs. Fremont. For what reason?

Choate. One known only to himself; but then that is not in the least uncommon, to delay the reading until a certain period elapses.

Mrs. Fremont. Do you think his deportment any way strange of late?

Choate. For the past week his countenance has been clouded as with a serious subject on his mind; but whether

the result of business depression or other causes I cannot
say.

Mrs. Fremont. He has these melancholy fits periodi-
cally.

Choate. Well the effect of a day's trading on the exchange is very exhausting. '

Enter Cicero.

Cicero. Missa Fremont, de supper room am ready fo
yo imspecshum.

Mrs. Fremont. Very well.—*Exit Cicero.*—You may
escort me, Senator.

Choate. You honor me.—*Exit.*

Enter Sumner and Lotta.

Sumner. Such are the affairs of men; the variations of
a career calculated to make any man thus experienced,
envious of one who possesses a home and friends.

Lotta. But has not your life had some brightness?

Sumner. Believe me when I say to-night has been the
happiest of my life. I have suffered much; and in what
few places I have had the fortune to be present where all
was going merry; and for the time being I felt a real taste
of enjoyment; a black cloud was sure to arise to cast its
gloom around me. So used to it have I become, I can believe myself capable of no happiness, but I must surely
suffer for it. I feel even to-night, a dread as if something would happen, I can guess not what, to mar the
evening's pleasure. *

Lotta. I fear you are too sensitive. I sympathize with
you. But some of your experiences have no doubt been
remarkable. Would you mind relating one?

Sumner. For me to relate some of my life's past chapters would be to spoil the evening for you; to shake your nerves. I would spare you that, Miss. Prescott.

Lotta. You have known the time you have had no place you could call home?

Sumner. I never knew the actual existence, to me of that, which is represented as a home. The world is my home. My father died many years ago; my mother when I was a child. Sorrowful indeed is the lot of one, who in childhood's years possesses not the parent's guidance. O, why was I not as fortunate as the thousands around me? No, I was doomed to struggle alone; and it has been a cycle of very bitter years. What! not tears, Miss Prescott? Pardon me, I did not intend—

Lotta. No, no, Mr. Sumner; only when you spoke, you unconsciously brought the recital to a simile: for my life has been as yours; I too am alone in the world.

Enter Lieut. and Hazel.

Hazel. What a charming tete-a-tete we must be having.

Lieut. We've been hunting the supper and ball-room for you, in every nook and corner.

Sumner. And here we're found.

Hazel. The Lieutenant has been expatiating on the beauties of friendship, in which he cites you, Mr. Sumner, as an example quite strong in that relation.

Lotta. We too were talking about home and friends.

Lieut. I have often wondered who is our best, our greatest friend, I mean the friend of friends.

Hazel. Why, what a question! our parents of course.

Sumner. That is debatable.

Lotta. What do you think, Mr. Sumner?

Sumner. You ask mine, tho' I voice opinions,
Don't call me cynic:
For I am not alone in like consideration.
As the Lieutenant holds my due respect
For he owns it surely, being my close friend;
And indeed you are all my friends,
Too valued to be lost; and quite properly
Exceptions to this radical opinion.
Friendship has a multitude of temptations.
This is a weary world, to one in distress,
To one ambitious; and in a measure
Of my experience, I have found one
Who in pleasure, in sickness, or in loneliness;
And moreover in all the sharper vicissitudes
And experiences of my life, was always for me,
And remained my advocate until the last: in fact,
My friend is the friend of any individual,
Who will treat this friend with due respect.

   Lieut. To whom do you refer?

   Lotta. Your father, Mr. Sumner?—*Shakes head.*

   Hazel. Your mother, without doubt?—*Shakes head.*

   Sumner. If you would know and yet you do, but have not made the extended acquaintance I have, and may your destiny forbid the necessity.—*Takes from his pocket and holds aloft a $20 gold piece.*—The great American eagle.

   Hazel. Why, Mr. Sumner, what a cynic you are!

   Sumner. There, I knew you'd cry cynicism.

   Lieut. Monte is right, for money will reach where friend or parent cannot find a way. I recall an incident that happened some years ago in an obscure frontier town in Arizona; La Paz, was the place, I believe. Monte was there though he did not witness the scene. It dealt with this question in a peculiar way.

Sumner. I remember the occurrence.—*Aside.*—I fixed the fool in time.

Lieut. I was sitting in the shade of the east wall of a low adobe, about half asleep; Monte had left but a few moments before, to go up to the plaza to see a bronco sale; when a thin, pale, haggard and roughly dressed man approached me in great excitement and cried out: "Keep away from him! shun his friendship! he will work you for all your worth, and leave you a wreck in body and in soul! he's the devil in a man! look at me and learn in time! once within his sway, it remains unbroken even with miles intervening! so it is with me. I feel his influence now, it is coming on again!—I am going!—my mind—my will—my reason!"—*Suddenly, with great self possession.*—"This desert has no mystery, allied to this of mine. What an actor I've become; two opposite parts I play with equal ease. At odd intervals I am a howling derangement; at others, the embodiment of the most tranquil and engaging comedy. Did I call him enemy? I'll traitor that assertion and call him friend, of mine, of yours; my favorite and most dearest associate; one who loves us for our souls, not our visible semblance. Remember my second reasoning has more in it than the first. Adios."— And he was gone.

Lotta. The poor man must have been insane.

Lieut. So I then believed, though his eyes were rational. It once occured to me that he might have been a hypnotic subject.

Hazel. How terrible!

Lieut. For at that time there was a report among the boys, that a tall man passing as a Mexican and with a Mexican's eye, had the power and used it: I never saw him and he disappeared very suddenly.

Sumner. I heard later he was killed over a poker game. He was trying to influence a player in his favor, but the opponent knowing him had a pistol and a will, so finis.

Lotta. So strange a life; so marvelous a country. We meet and miss many a bewildering theme.

Sumner. And such is life as I have seen it;
I would venture to state – that
Expose to the light of vision and knowledge,
Let stock forth the hidden skeletons in the lives
Of some of our social companions:
Then stop and note the result.
It would stagger the unthinking and confiding
And strengthen the wildest exaggerations of a cynic.
Great tragedies are within a short radius
Of our sight—impenetrable to us:
Dissimulation shields too well:
Except when some crisis brings them forth,
They remain hidden, but rarely suspicioned.
Our whole social existence is a vast network
Of hypocrisy: barring that much despised and
Cried-down talent, life would have but little spice.
I would say that of him who can dissemble
Successfully, Nature has conferred a priceless gift.
Why the weeps of the crocodile in figurative speech
Do flood the world of eyes, at times:
Would I be so coarse of fineness of assertion
To include them all?   No; but many eyes
Do well o'er of the watery hypocrisy, that makes

The cheeks a river's bed o'er which
To flow the volume of hypocritical show,
Seen, called, supposed, as honest tears.
Tears—better some than none, as goes the occasion.

Hazel. Some events in your life, Mr. Sumner, must have been most severe, to cause you to expound such cold philosophy.

Lotta. Well, you know the time is looked forward to, by many, when all things will run smoothly, and all will be happy.

Sumner. The man that hopes for the millennium, the great era of universal happiness, has a very poor conception of the plots and combinations of human life. He should study human nature just a little, and throw in a few thoughts on the world's history.

Lieut. Such is life. It's philosophy and philosophy; a creed and a saying; rules, proverbs, commentaries and commandments: it's talk and argue; a question put; a question answered, sometimes not; without end: we are all jumping-jacks to destiny.

Enter Choate and Mrs. Fremont.

Lotta. Dancing over? We have been having such an interesting little lecture on friendships, dissimulation, the millennium and jumping-jacks; the time has passed unnoticed: it surely is not late?

Choate. No, early yet; only an intermission; the musicians wish a slight refreshment for their pains.

Sumner. Quite deserving; a sweet compensation for sweet sounds.

Mrs. Fremont. I am more than pleased with their selections to-night. .

Enter other dancers.—Exit Sumner unobserved by stage.—Enter Mrs. Kelton.

Lieut. I would say, Mrs. Fremont, that this reception will be acknowledged one of the most successful of the season.

Choate. Mrs. Fremont is noted for her success in all things social.—*Enter more guests.*

Mrs. Kelton. Senator, this evening recalls old Washington days. This, you know is my first winter in the city in many years.

Choate. Then I am sure you will enjoy it, so delightful is the winter season East. This time last year I was visiting in San Francisco, and wonderful climate as it is, one misses the romance of the sleigh-bells, snow and bare-limbed trees. Evergreens are Nature's fashion in California.

Enter Fremont. Goes to (L) unnoticed, first acts strangely, then performs a grotesque dance. In center door stands Sumner directing his movements by hypnotic power, also unseen by stage; being partially concealed by drapery.

Sumner. Aside. The crisis is at hand.

Mrs. Fremont. The West is grand, and takes first place for scenery of diversified Nature; and that is all: if you would live, you must live East.

Lieut. I disagree with you there, Mrs. Fremont; though I have been stationed the greater part of my time in the Southwest, I feel calculated from my travels to speak of the more northern states. The people of the West are like their great mountains, rivers and plains, in using a simile; the most open-hearted, generous, frank and social branch of the great American family. Society in the West, though in its infancy as regards old and conservative traditions, is laying a foundation for social advancement, culture and progress, that will never be outranked by society east of the Rockies.

Choate. Yes, I am of——*Crash.—During last words of Lieut. Cicero enters with tray and wine glasses; sees Fremont; stops, looks on in wonder, drops tray as Choate speaks. All turn and see Fremont.*

Mrs. Fremont. Why this burlesque! Jackson? The ball-room is near and more appropriate to such——

Fremont. Stops short, eyes her wildly.—Silence! Would you disturb the last happy hours of a man condemned to everlasting companionship with Mephisto?

Mrs. Fremont. Cicero, remove your master, he is ill.

Cicero. Advances carefully and appears frightened.

Fremont. Points finger at him and thunders out.

Black man! ebon-hued slave!
Namesake of the illustrious Roman!
(A darkened honor to his memory,)
Let not your charcoaled hand, rest
Authoritatively on the sacred person of the white!

Cicero. Nods head, steps back.—Yes sah, yes sah.

Mrs. Fremont. Cicero! did you hear me? Jackson— *Advances toward Fremont, who waves her back.*

Fremont. Woman, use diplomacy; keep in practice
The master talent of your sex.
You understand not my mood. I stand
On the threshold of the unknown world:
Too long I've lived to suffer a weight
Of misery, born of an injustice done
To other men. My liberty at last, O soul
Of this most racked and tortured brain,
Fly away to—*Suddenly and calmly*—what?

The service of the Devil,—*Excitedly.*
Who would in the orthodox fashion
Gather me in to feed the furnace fires of Hell!
No! no! it is not so! begone evil teachings
To my youngest years! I am for Heaven!
. I see the light breaking! my soul is free.—*Stops suddenly,
then very deliberately.*

> Here's to you and yours,
> Here's to theirs and mine;
> I know all will join me,
> And drink these healths
> In this royal old wine,
> O, learn to die in time.

*Drinks contents of a vial concealed in hand.—Dies.—
Confusion.—Exit Mrs. Fremont, fainting, assisted by
Lotta and Hazel.—Exit Mrs. Kelton.—Others remain.
Lieut. To Cicero.—A doctor quick.—Exit Cicero.*

Enter Sumner.

Sumner. What is this commotion about? What has
happened? Who did this?
Choate. Suicide, while temporarily insane—prussic acid.
Sumner. Ladies and Gentlemen:
You have witnessed a most tragic episode.
An incident has transformed this mirthful evening
To a night blasted by the most terrible guest
That could visit an assemblage. A visitor
Always dreaded; usually unthought of; yet
Has been welcomed: but not this night.
O, Death, unbidden,—*Aside.*—Yet I did bid.
Why will you come unheralded?
Mysterious personage, what countless shadowy

Ways you tax the soul, (if there be a soul?)
With the burden of a flight to the unknown sphere.
We all in this life's fleeting interval
Must acknowledge you a power:
Some here, have no doubt held temporary
Association with you before.   Extending
Through a most stormy and eventful career;
Though not in time spanning as many winters
As has silvered the brow of the gentleman on my left:
  Referring to Choate.
I have observed many heartrending scenes.
My way has often led me within the circle
Of solemn sound, tolled forth from many
A slow-measured and deep-toned bell;
And as I advanced nearer within the radius;
I stood at last beneath the vaulted roof
And sculptured dome of the sacred edifice:
Environed by that hushed stillness
That is a respect to the presence of the dead.
But I've seen no scene, to me so sad as this.
Once when I was down, a victim
In the iron grasp of adversity; verging   .
On self-destruction; the man now inanimate
Before me, said: "You require help,
Here it is," an act burnt in my memory
As with a brand: it left in me a profound
Feeling of gratitude.   Now is a crying moment.
Here lies my friend, so still: shortly ago
He walked among his guests honored and respected
By all; now will elapse the season of a week,
And he is forgotten to the rushing world about:
For he was a moneyed man and that was all.   To me,

He was a virtuous man; to the world in general
The same; to himself, to his own private thoughts,
He might not have known its meaning;
He may have called it policy.
His virtues to me were many, and of one, generosity,
I find with the majority, a trait most scarce:
To some, that virtue of his so highly
Thought of by me, might not hold good as well.
Old friend, may the coming of the blessing
Of everlasting peace, reflect upon you
That love of mine, for you; as Death has left
To me its memory, no longer its application.

Lieut. Aside to Choate.—Such a scene as we have
witnessed, touches one's finer and nobler feelings, and
tends to strengthen one's confidence in human nature.

Choate. I do not wish my confidence in human nature
strengthened, for to-morrow would only shatter it: it might
strengthen it for the individual, but not for human nature
in general.

END OF ACT II.

ACT III.

Hazel. And do you think, Grandma, that Mama will not recover from the shock? It is now one month today since poor Papa's death.

Mrs. Kelton. Your mother is seriously ill, my child; I fear will go hard with her: ever since that terrible collision two years ago, you know she never was the same. Dr. Allopath told me yesterday it was an organic affection of the heart, and he is treating her accordingly; so hereafter she must avoid all excitement; but being so ambitious, she will find it a struggle to renounce the position held so long.

Hazel. O, what can I do? what can be done, to make her life a quieter one?

Mrs. Kelton. I fear nothing; she will have her way: but possibly she may realize her condition, and use more care.

Hazel. I do hope so. Tell me, Grandma; what was the trouble of long years ago, that worried Papa so?

Mrs. Kelton. Only some difficulty Jackson had regarding a mining claim, in which John had an interest. John was a good man, but had too much the spirit of the wanderer. Now ask no more questions; it's a past you should and shall know nothing about.

Enter Cicero with card.

Hazel.   Reads.—Mr. Sumner!—Show him here.—*Exit Cicero.*

Enter Sumner.

Sumner.   Mrs. Kelton, Miss Emory, I am happy to see you.   I hope you are both quite well.

Hazel.   Granma is well and I am as usual.

Sumner.   What news from Lenox. is Mrs. Fremont improving?

Mrs. Kelton.   Yes, slowly; though the past month has been very trying, she requiring absolute quiet; a month more we hope for a great change in her favor.   I must see to certain household duties, so will leave you for a time.—*Exit.*

Sumner.   And in the interval of time elapsing, we'll try and put to good account.   Miss Emory, have you any recollection of your father, who died in the Southwest?

Hazel.   Of my father I know very little, he left home when I was a child.

Sumner.   I knew once an individual by that name, who cherished me with a father's love; this was long ago; the idea occured to me they might be in some way related. The name is not common.   And you are the only child then?

Hazel.   No, I had a brother four years older, who accompanied my father on his Western tour.

Sumner.   May I ask his name?

Hazel.   His name was Walter, but you would not know him, you have never met him.   He too died of fever in Sonora.

Sumner. That is indeed sad. Did Mr. Fremont know your father, may I ask?

Hazel. Really, Mr. Sumner, you must excuse me, this subject is most painful to me; and I can truthfully add I know almost nothing of my father's and brother's history.

Sumner. I must be mistaken; the one I had reference to lived in England; I met him when I was in Liverpool.— *Aside.* –No information there; if all women knew so little how sacred would be our secrets.—*To Hazel.*—I trust, Miss Emory, you have taken no offense to my inquiries?

Hazel. Not in the least, Mr. Sumner.

Sumner. Then we continue friends.

Enter Lieut.

Lieut. Ah! found you Miss Emory; Monte, I am glad to see you.

Sumner. Good day, Lieutenant.

Lieut. Mrs. Kelton said I would find you here.

Enter Lotta.

Lotta. Good afternoon, gentlemen.

Lieut. Good afternoon, Miss Prescott.

Sumner. I am glad to see you are looking better.— *Plucks rose and presents to Lotta.*—Accept this; its shade is a delicate contrast to the slight paleness that marks your features.

Lotta. Thanks; would all roses were as sweet and sweetly given. I am in better spirits to-day, but time, even though short, will mark our countenances worn, as the influence of the sadness undergone, breaks way its sombre bonds.

Enter Mrs. Kelton.

Sumner. Was I not promised, Mrs. Kelton, a peep at some of your old family heir-looms, those interesting relics of a past generation, and the old Virginia days?

Mrs. Kelton. Yes, indeed; you shall see them all; come right along, Lotta you may assist me.

Sumner. Are you not coming, too?

Hazel. No, the old are old to me; the Lieutenant and I have pored over musty tomes, spinning wheels and quaint medallions before, many times.

Lieut. We'll leave you to the examination. Mrs. Kelton and Miss Prescott are most entertaining in their description of historical articles.—*Exit Lotta, Sumner and Mrs. Kelton.*

Lieut. Hazel, since last I was with you, I have experienced the untold agonies of one in love; visions of your mother's refusal kept rising up before me.

Hazel. You should not be in love.

Lieut. Little sweetheart of mine, you know full well were I not in love with you, you'd be the first to wish it.

Hazel. Ah, indeed, are you so handsome then?

Lieut. That's as you place me. And did you not, I would not be making love to the sweetest girl I've ever met.

Hazel. And you think me so?

Lieut. I've so told you, wrote you now going on the thousandth time. Yes, Hazel sweet, Hazel sweeter, Hazel sweetest of them all!

Hazel. Bewitching as those dark-eyed, beautiful, romantic daughters of the tropics; the Spanish senoritas— Ray?

Lieut. Come now, Hazel, that's rough; because I happened to have lived a few months in close proximity to Mexico, you imagine I must be enraptured with Spanish loveliness: just you go to Mexico once, and see well the so-called charms of the Mexican women, and you will return and acknowledge to me how pretty you are.

Hazel. To you, Ray, I may be pretty and sweet, as you have often told me; but others' opinions of the object of your admiration, might not rise to your standard.

Lieut. Hazel, darling, it is impossible for the criticisms of others to differ from my own.

Hazel. But suppose——

Lieut. What? Mama objects?

Hazel. Objection always on your mind? Yes, what if the word is no?

Lieut. Though no it be, I am determined even by desperate measures to make no synonymous with yes; a task not always difficult and often accomplished. But I cannot believe Mrs. Fremont capable of causing us such pain.

Hazel. You do not know Mama, she is ruled by policy; a virtue, the cause of much that appears heartless, but has an end in view. It is only today Grandma said Mama had laid down the law that reads for Lotta and I, wealth must be our husbands, matters not has wealth grey hairs or the idiotic expression of a gilded youth of fallowed brains.

Lieut. I shall not have it no; though I am at the orders of ranked superiors, to do duty where and when they bid; I shall resign and enter mercantile life; less lofty as to asperations that surround it, but more for me in keeping with the times. The pursuit of increased gold lace and brass buttons, I'll change for the seeking of gold notes and silver dollars.

Hazel. But I love that uniform so.

Lieut. I know it darling, it helped me win you.

Hazel. It did not.

Lieut. Show me the woman that admires not the soldier's plumes.

Hazel. How wise you are about what attracts the feminine eye. You have brown eyes, Ray.

Lieut. And you red lips.—*Kisses her.*

Hazel. Did I say for you to kiss me?

Lieut. Well, modest young ladies never ask, For what modest young men never take.

Hazel. Then you are far from modest.

Lieut. No, I am a soldier, and as you love soldiers— *Kisses her.*

Hazel. I shall never ask for you to kiss me.

Lieut. Not necessary; consent is given in three ways: by silence, in a look, and by a word.

Hazel. You torment. Do you know I believe some one else is getting spoony here lately.

Lieut. You don't mean to say I am, do you, darling?

Hazel. Any one can see it, love; but I placed in comparison to you Mr. Sumner; he shows his admiration for Lotta, O so often.

Lieut. More than I for you?

Hazel. He is not as sweet.

Lieut. How can you tell?

Hazel. How could he be?

Lieut. Lotta's views are different.

Hazel. Well, there may be two brides yet in Grace Church.

Lieut. It may be Grace Church, it may be the office of some country justice. I saw he lost his heart the first night he came here; why he could monopolize a young ladies' company to the exclusion of others, in about as artistic a manner as one might wish to admire.

Hazel. Yes, he was with me a great deal.

Lieut. Now, you can't make me jealous, so don't try.

Hazel. How susceptible men are; I wonder if he will tell her of it?

Lieut. If Sumner does not, he is losing his courage fast. he is the nerviest man I have ever known; stops at nothing to gain a point: why one day in Casa Grande—

Hazel. Yes, these brave men on the field or among their fellows, or in some great emergency, are as a rule such terribly timid creatures when they go to do a little love-making. Now you remember, dear, when you first—

Lieut. Yes, darling, that—that's all right—I was—

Hazel. O! I am a soldier.

Lieut. Here comes Mrs. Kelton; I heard her voice on the stairs. Luck to the lottery of a guess, she is alone.

Hazel. I must go, I heard the postman's whistle, a letter from Mama.—*Starts to go.*

Lieut. *Holds her back.*—Just one more.

Hazel. *Demurely.*—You usually ask for two, and take a dozen.

Lieut. Never fear, I will take a trial balance.—*Kissing her as Mrs. Kelton enters.*

Mrs. Kelton. I can understand why you take no interest in spinning wheels, medallions and cracked china.

Hazel. O, Grandma!—*Exit.*

Lieut. Mrs. Kelton, you have fairly caught us.

Mrs. Kelton. Tut-tut, it's nothing; I've known it a long time.

Lieut. I am happy then in the knowledge, you look at it favorably.

Mrs. Kelton. Don't let me see too much, you might make me envious; O, if I was'nt eighty years of age.

Lieut. Fond of a joke still, Grandma? Do you know I fear Mrs. Fremont will oppose the match; even though Mr. Fremont gave his consent before he died; I am not wealthy.

Mrs. Kelton. When I was young, though money had great influence, worth always received respectful recognition. I know you to be worthy of Hazel's love, and shall assist you all it's possible for me to do.

Lieut. Mrs. Kelton, I thank you; as I fought the Indians, so I shall fight for Hazel; with a strong determination to win.

Mrs. Kelton. Let us hope we will succeed. But do you think there exists ties stronger than mere friendship between Lotta and Mr. Sumner? I never noticed anything until up-stairs a short time ago, when we were looking at the heir-looms; Lotta seemed very anxious about my pet canaries, she thought James had neglected to feed them.

Lieut. Ha! ha! as I suspected: old tricks, I have been right there— -

Mrs. Kelton. I am well aware of it. It used to be pet canaries with Hazel, now Lotta is becoming interested: those birds of mine never looked so well fed before. They have about stopped singing.

Lieut. Monte is a noble fellow.

Mrs. Kelton. I like him, his character appears exceptional.

Enter Cicero.

Cicero. De dry goods man am come wid de samples,
Missa Kelton.—*Exit.*

Mrs. Kelton. Then I will send down Mr. Sumner to
keep you company; the girls I shall need with me for a
short time.—*Exit.*

Lieut. As you will, Mrs. Kelton.
Life, life; a yes, a no, at times, completes our destiny;
Is the die of our fate: matters not the power
Of the being, from whom we are forced
To take this aye or nay, it holds good,
Unless a crisis arrives to sunder
The spell for either ends of a question.
And here's an unwelcome instance,
Wherein I am forced to take the nay,
And the sundering crisis 'll not arrive.—
Takes from pocket a paper. Enter Sumner.

Sumner.—What! old fellow, you look bluer than the
blues.

Lieut. Thinking, only wondering; an idea that I mentioned to Hazel, has just come to mind with redoubled
force; that has scattered blue fancies far from my disposition: though the countenance molds in looks, in keeping
with the thoughts as a rule: and deep thoughts and blues
appear with much the same marks.

Sumner. Thoughts worth thinking should always
receive attention: what is the title to yours, Miss Emory?

Lieut. Yes, and the idea; I shall resign my commission.

Sumner. No! Why, what's the merit of the trouble?

Lieut. Hands letter to Sumner.—Read.

Sumner. Still a lieutenant? Come, that's discouraging, but don't——

Lieut. That's what it is to have swell and indifferent relations; two of which occupy influential positions in the War Department: I reckoned on a pull.

O my relations,sweet relations, what worthies you are;
And how I despise you, but cannot apprise you,
For fear my chances it 'd mar; there's a fact.

Sumner. In all places, and of all faces or races,
Relations at times the most despicable are.

Lieut. Give me a friend for a relation,
To my approbation; but never a relation that far,
That's as a friend.
No, there is no money in my salary, there's more in mines.
I located a claim or two during my campaigns, that will pay development. I never noted the force of the money question till of late.

Sumner. That which is good fortune does not always
Appear to us at first sight in agreeable aspect.
Speculate; there lies fortune's greatest favors.
Go on the street and believe not all you hear;
For many speculators omit the S, in the title
Of their occupation: use care with such.
Still if possible, never offend a speculator;
Keep his friendship on the issue of a smile;
And fail not to remark the fact,
That though he may be penniless to-day,
To-morrow might strike the opposite in his fortunes.
No, hold him dear particularly does he place
Greater stress on his own opinions than on points.

And I'll give you two points now; in stock dealings
With others, always be fortified with the newest
Informations, (from where got, matters not).
To keep them in an anxious state for a something
Yet to come. We hope the stock—we stock on hope.
Also; a man you'd ask favors of, if possible,
Interest in a scheme, interesting to his pocket:
Watch him love you.   There's few exceptions.
And push quick acquaintance with some insider.
 Lieut. Done, Arizona and Uncle Sam, adieu,
I'll plunge Wall Street through.
 Sumner. I don't see but what such a course
Would be a good selection.
But remember, that while you are down
To thunder all your works and talents,
Also acting modest;
And, when on the platform of success,
Shape your deportment to your moods.
Success to your certificates.
Tell me, what of Miss Emory?
 Lieut. Monte, I'll have that girl if I have to elope
with her.
 Sumner. What a change from your old ideas. "O, I
prefer bachelor's hall; you are so free and independent."
When you are in Miss Emory's company you look the
very spirit of Garibaldi, ha! ha!
 Lieut. I was wrong, but don't you believe in marriage?
 Sumner. Of marriage I have a doubt if there ever has
been or ever will be a more ennobling social institution.
 Lieut. As they say out West, "Pard, them'ar's my sen-
timents." Possibly I may require assistance in my love
affair; can I count—

Sumner. As Kent to Lear, so I to you.

Lieut. Gracias amigo! Say old boy, tell me, are you in love?

Sumner. I love her the most, who knows me the least. Yes, Lotta is the gentle answer of a wish, I shall marry her.

Lieut. Bueno, bueno, Senor. When we were in Arizona, though we passed through some strange and severe trials, still I did not have the opportunity to know you as I wished, now I want to see more of you. You have a cool confidence I do not possess; Nature's slight, not West Point's.

Sumner. Aside.—Those who have seen more of me often wish they had seen less.

Lieut. Had Hazel a big brother now, he could win his mother over. I know she will object: but as no big brother exists I will vote you to the vacancy.

Sumner. Elected. I will be Hazel's brother for she'll never have another.

Lieut. I must tell Hazel you have found a sister.

Sumner. Don't; she will ask you who I have been proposing to.

Enter Lotta.

Lotta. I have decided on a shade for the new parlor hangings; Hazel is still uncertain.

Lieut. I guess I shall go and help her out.—*Exit.*

Sumner. Go, Lieutenant, you admire the beautiful—*Looks at Lotta; eyes meet--Lotta goes to window and looks out on falling snow.—Sumner follows, and with eyes on Lotta finishes sentence.*--And so do I. How beautiful the snow,

Falling so lightly, so silently:
Snow, ' Pure as snow,' as goes the saying;
Such a character makes its finding difficult;
But when placed, is amongst womankind
Found. Of men, it does rarely exist.
Were all our characters spotless
As the driven snow; the world would be
The materialized idea of the creeds;
Quite too monotonous, not fit to live in.

Lotta. Once again, Mr. Sumner; why what cynical
ideas compose your philosophy. I am going to teach you
ethics more in keeping with the general views.

Sumner. Would that you could, Miss Prescott; but I
fear your task will be discouragingly difficult. It would
have to necessarily upset the principles bitter experience
has taught me.

Lotta. I am in sympathy with you, Mr. Sumner.
Your life must have been a sad experience, your philosophy
declares the fact: none but those who have born a weight
of sorrow could speak as that: I too have suffered; but I
know did we measure our sorrows, as blade to blade in a
duel, you'd win the point of greater anguish.

Sumner. My way has been exceptional, others do not
suffer as I have suffered.

Lotta. Fortitude will win in the end.

Sumner. There is a virtue often made too virtuous. It
may win, it may fail; even when a lifetime of respect, it
has received from some poor confiding mortal.

Lotta. Then what is certain?

Sumner. With a few exceptions, all is doubt; and the
world usually chooses with few exceptions to believe itself
one of the exceptions; in view of Fate.— *Walks to a palm*

tree.—What a contrast, these waving palms, fan-leaved and thousand-ribbed; reflecting the light green tropic shades; look without; snow, ice and bitter cold: one warm, balmy, soft, fit representative of romantic climes; the influence of the other cold and cheerless, sways in its own way. O, a Mexican night: what memories, romances, traditions.

Lotta. You love the South?

Sumner. More than words can describe. The South is the land of the sentimentalist, the dreamer, the poet. I would to you, in poor words describe most complicated feelings in a poetic way; an admonition not to wish, and a question of the wisdom of the warning.

Lotta. I should like to hear it.

Sumner. Draws close to her, both seated on a rustic bench.

> Wish not to be,
> What thou canst not be:
> Yet, how wouldst thou know
> Thou canst not be
> What thou wouldst wish to be?

Lotta. It is pretty; what would you wish to be?

Sumner. Cannot you guess?

Lotta. Shakes head wonderingly.

Sumner. The lover of a soul, so sweet, so sympathetic, so beautiful; of one in form and feature so lovable in my eyes.

Lotta. Slightly hesitating.—Of whom? Who can be so beautiful to you?

Sumner. Business.—Does he exist who has a better right than I?

Lotta. No, Monte.

Sumner. Kisses her.—I've won! I've won!

Lotta. Archly.—Do all men love women so? Is—is
it—all such ecstasy of feeling—too difficult to describe—
but—so—delightful?

Sumner. Some, not all. It depends upon the lover
and the loved; the passion, the soul. Even villains love
women just as much as so-called good and honest men,
and they sometimes make ten-fold better lovers and sweet-
hearts.

Lotta. I don't think they could be sweeter than you—
could it be you are a villain?

Sumner. I must acknowledge it; yes Lotta; I am of
a desperate type; I have stolen; I am a highwayman; the
guilt of embezzlement is weighted upon me. So I shall
continue; it is to the nature of my education, so firmly im-
planted that all prisons, creeds and pledges, would not
restrain the master passion of my character.

Lotta. O Monte! What have you done?

Sumner. Stolen your love and kisses. Don't tell,
Lotta.

Lotta. You tease.

Enter Cicero with card.

Lotta. Reads.—Mr. Bowie, Chihuahua.—*Pronounced
broadly.*—Show the gentleman in.—*Exit Cicero.*

Sumner. That's a good joke, ha! ha! I must give you
a few lessons in Spanish, Lotta love. Chihuahua.—*Giv-
ing proper pronunciation.*—The two last h's are silent,
the i is an e, u is an oo, and a is an ah.—*Aside.*—Who is
Bowie? and from Chihuahua.— *Walks to (L.)*

Lotta. Cicero misunderstood me.   He is bringing the gentleman here, instead of the reception room.

Cicero. Announces.—Mistah Bowie.—*Exit.*

Enter Bowie.—*Starts slightly on seeing Lotta.*

Bowie. May I see Mrs. Fremont?

Sumner turns when Bowie speaks; gives a sharp glance at Bowie, who does not see him, and says very coldly and cooly.—*Aside.*—My father!

Lotta. Mama is not in town; 1 do not expect her for two weeks yet; she has been very ill.

Bowie. Are you—are you Miss Emory, may I ask?

Lotta. No, I am her cousin.   If you wish to see her I will send—*Starts to ring bell.*

Sumner. Steps forward quickly, hand extended, perfectly composed.

Bowie. Monte! Monte Em—

Sumner. Interrupts quickly.—Mr. Bowie, I am glad to see you; when your card was sent in I did not dream it was that of my superintendent and old acquaintance. Allow me, Miss Prescott; Mr. Bowie.

Lotta. Mr. Bowie, I am pleased to meet you.

Bowie. Miss Prescott, I am delighted.   It quite startled me to meet here the owner of the mine I represent.

Sumner. Aside to Bowie.—My name is Mr. Sumner, from Tombstone.

Lotta. One does meet old friends under such queer circumstances and in such unlikely places.

Sumner. Yes indeed.

Enter Cicero with card.

Lotta. Takes card.—Senator Choate has called.   Show

him to the library, Cicero.—*Exit Cicero.*—Gentlemen if you will excuse me for a short time.

Bowie and Sumner.　Certainly.

Exit Lotta.

Sumner.　Father! Dad! O, my father! is this reality? Here! you! after all these years?—and I,—I thought you dead,—I the poor fatherless, homeless wanderer.

Bowie.　Monte, my boy, and I thought you dead, I too the homeless vagabond, the outcast. This is too much! And this is the ending of a Hell on earth, to live as I have lived? To find my boy at. last, nine, long, weary years. To realize the truth is to ask an injustice of my understanding. I saw you boy taken captive, and knew the tortures you would undergo; but you survived, lived.

Sumner.　Then my eyes too did descry a mirage? it has continued a nine years delusion. I sighted as we turned to go, you left for dead upon the field; and Death made not its coming, another reaped.

Bowie.　I feigned death and by that escaped; but was badly wounded. The band hurried in their work, urged by a detachment in pursuit, or torture would have prolonged as I thought the surely condemned life's spark. No doubt we have been near each other many times since. The Greasers abandoned the chase; and the Indians soon disappeared among the hills, bearing you.

Sumner.　Yes, I was held captive for three years; became a bandit, a calling forced upon me. Ah! but I have suffered! I know what it is. I escaped eventually, and have leased the world for my home ever since.

Bowie.　My poor boy, I too have suffered; how hard is life, how merciless is Fate.

Sumner. Fate has taught me to be merciless; O man, your Hell is right here on this earth.

Bowie. Monte, it is a bitter life. But what brings you here? in that question lies my greatest surprise. This is the house of your mother; my mission is to see her, recall a few forgotten memories, and reckon with the man who stole from me everything that I had to look forward to in this life. I've spent six years in a Mexican prison on charges barren of a just cause—

Sumner. A Mexican prison! God!

Bowie. And was liberated only a month ago. Previous to my incarceration the three years were but a record of lost or unanswered letters and aimless wanderings in Lower California, or I would have settled with Fremont years before. Where is he now? I want to see him.—*Draws pistol.*

Sumner. Takes pistol.—A fine weapon; it's polished barrel gleams ominously; many are the scores you and your fellows have wiped out. You'll serve a judge's ends in Arizona, but not here. This country is too civilized.— *Aside.*—Here the eye was a greater power than the noisy weapon.—*Returning it to Bowie.*—It is worthless for your purpose.

Bowie. Why, what is the matter with it? I tested it only a week ago in San Antonio, Texas. I shall kill Fremont.

Sumner. He's dead.

Bowie. Dead! dead you say? no,
It can't be possible I'm cheated; this long
Wished for reckoning now'll be naught.
In the weary hours of my captivity,
It seemed that for end, there was no end;

I watched the dial of a little watch
Kept secreted in my cell:
And prayed that those slowly-turning hands
Would creep on at a quicker pace, and time
Would slip away in keeping with the action.
One hope alone consoled me; that, to seek
Fremont, and cry out at the meeting
As has been done in cases similar,
" Vengeance! vengeance is mine!"
I was liberated; I have sought and not found
The subject of my thoughtful moods;
I cannot say now, " Vengeance is mine."

Sumner. *Aside.*—No, it is mine, but the honor will
stretch for two. *To Bowie.*—No, no stain shall blot the
old record; he died one month ago to-day; committed suicide in a fit of temporary insanity: so the papers said.

Bowie. Disappointment, you and my future are of the
same fraternity. Monte, how are you fixed? Though I
was so far broke three weeks ago, that for being obliged
to ride the brakes, a division; a rascally justice of Flagstaff
called me a Hobo; ordered me to leave town in six hours;
and a worthless half-breed Moqui intimated that my game
of poker 'd not stand analysis. Yet I made a stake in
Albuqerque at Faro and Three-card Monte. Remember
how you received your name? Recollect how you won
fifty dollars from Juan Torres, in El Paso, the night
before we left for Chihuahua?

Sumner. Yes, father, all. I am well fixed; I recently
received a large sum of money from some mines in Tombstone; my regular dividends: and also, just previous to his
death, I remarked the remorse of Fremont; a change to a
mood that favored much my claims. He made a will and

by its provisions, forgetfulness of my right was not countenanced.

Bowie. Fremont repent! Is it possible? It was time. I am glad you got something out of him. But your mother, how did she receive you?

Sumner. Received unrecognized; for I have changed in fifteen years. Was introduced by a friend of mine, Lieutenant Silverton; Fremont did not tell her of my being here, and he died directly after. Though originally Walter Emory, I have lived under the assumed name of Sumner for years; keeping only the nickname Monte, you used to call me by. None know me here; I do not wish it, and for awhile favor me and remain incog; therefore to me before others you are Mr. Bowie; to me alone, my own father. But how came you to introduce yourself as Mr. Bowie?

Bowie. I was afraid I'd not be admitted did I give the name of Emory.

Sumner. Your foresight is a credit to your judgment; your fortune then in that is mine as well. Will not Mrs. Kelton recognize you?

Bowie. What! the old woman still alive?

Sumner. Yes, and resident here; good for ten years yet. The past has made few changes with you, still have a beard I see.

Bowie. Where I was confined they did not shave the prisoners; it was too much trouble.

Sumner. Leave it to me, I shall arrange it. Inform the girls the reason that you came to see Mrs. Fremont was to inquire concerning me: though it was a strange entrance.

Bowie. I am to see Hazel then? She will not recognize me.

Sumner. I think not, but forget not my caution; you are Mr. Bowie from Chihuahua.

Bowie. I'll be cautious.

Sumner. John Emory died nine years ago, as did the boy.

Bowie. They did.

Enter Lotta, Hazel and Lieut.

Sumner. Miss Emory, Lieutenant, my friend Mr. Bowie from Chihuahua, the superintendent of the Aztec's Legacy, a mine in which I have an interest.

Lieut. Mr. Bowie.

Hazel. Mr. Bowie, I am delighted. This is a freak of destinations and of homes; Lieutenant Silverton from Las Nogales and Fort Yuma, Mr. Sumner from Tombstone, and I again have the pleasure of an acquaintance with another resident of the Southwest.

Bowie. Though a resident of Southern Arizona Districts for a time, many of my years have been spent on Mexican soil; the land of the cactus.

Lotta. What romance surrounds that far-away country: the names are glamoured o'er strangely and weirdly; Apaches, Tombstones, and long Spanish and Indian words.

Lieut. Ah! Apaches and tombstones, two of a kind which fail to ultimately meet until a long record of treachery and crime bring the extremes to one completed tale.

Sumner. What a pensive thought for Arizonians; all Apaches under tombstones.

Bowie. Aside to Sumner.—And this beautiful girl is my daugh'er?

Sumner. That is my sister.

Enter Mrs. Kelton. Bowie turns to one side on seeing her, and Sumner exclaims:

Sumner. I thought I saw a mouse there.

Ladies shriek, Lotta and Hazel jump on chairs, Mrs. Kelton grasps skirts and exits. Lieut. looks for mouse and Sumner stands unconcerned.

Hazel. O, where? where is it? Look out Ray!

Lotta. Cicero! ring for Cicero! Take it away! Mr. Sumner, get on the table. Look out Mr. Bowie.

Sumner. Laughs.—Ah Ladies, I ask your pardon, I see it now; it was but a draught that rustled the tassel on the portiere. You have nothing to fear, the coast is clear. But, come Mr. Bowie, we must be going; it is late. *Ladies still on chairs.*

Lotta. What a fright you gave us. Are you real sure the little creature is not there, Monte—Mr. Sumner?

Sumner. Quite positive. *Helps her off chair, Lieut. helps Hazel off.*

Bowie. Aside.—She calls him Monte, then corrects herself: so there dips the lead.

Sumner. Aside to Bowie; all start to go.—The ruse succeeded; the old lady did not see you.

END OF ACT III.

ACT IV.

Scene.—*The Library. Two months later.*

Enter Sumner, shown in by Cicero.

Sumner. Today the will's seals are broken;
I shall make known my real identity;
It will contrast oddly with the role I've played;
But being fertile in the formation of excuses,
I can trust my future to the ready thought.
As I have noted my mother's character,
My actual home-coming promises scanty revelry;
But the forward question of such an hour,
How is it all to end?

*Enter Lotta with flowers; arranges in a vase on center
table; does not see Sumner, who takes seat in one corner.*

Lotta. Sweet Amaranth, fabled flower unfading;
Be my love's companion forever, and its simile;
For you, though mythical, will never die.
Fictioned Amaranth, receive the respect
I wish to bestow, while in this sentimental mood.
Flowering Amaranth, my love for him though like
To you in length of years, is still dissimilar;
For my love exists, and you do not.
How could the Amaranth that's naught, die?
There is naught then to die in that:
A slip of reason in that question.

Its memory may seek the burial vaults
Of long forgotten imaginings; and there ends
What then exists. But hold, I'll place you
Real, alive, to bloom companion to my love:
Not of earth and water nursed, vain regret to sigh
For what cannot exist: does there not exist enough?
Here is a thought, grateful to this moment;
Did it live; a living flower; a beauteous plant;
Its fabled leaves be live; representative
Of the imagined one whereof I spoke;
T'would be subject to the evils of its fellows,
And prey to death. The rude hand to break it,
The negligent hand to water it, if I away,
Would kill it. Then what becomes
My love's synonym? Non-existent with me,
Perhaps elsewhere, but the particular one is gone,
The one I treasured most.
No, back to the mind's fantastic realms,
You fabled flower, you must not live to die,
But live to never die.
Beautiful Amaranth, my love; a twain, the same.

Sumner. Who is he?

Lotta. Why! I thought I was alone. Did you just
come in.

Sumner. Heard it all. But tell me, Lotta, who is he?

Enter Hazel.

Sumner. Good afternoon, Miss Emory, another stormy
day finds me here.

Hazel. And you are indeed welcome; what is the
latest news from Chihuahua? I have quite fallen in love
with that marvelous country of the Southwest. I think

Mr. Bowie is such a pleasant person, so well informed; I
have taken quite a fancy to him. Do you know he bears
a striking resemblance to an old photograph of my father.

Sumner. Indeed, Mr. Bowie is certainly calculated to
prove himself interesting; he has traveled much and had
many startling adventures. Miss Prescott, you—

Hazel. Why don't you call her Lotta? Mr. Sumner,
I shall leave and give you a chance.—*Exit laughing.*

Lotta. Hazel, you should be ashamed—

Sumner. Why?
Let others know your love is my pride;
I could eloquently declare it to all the world,
And yet not express the happiness of owning
Such a possession. Love, love;
As an exponent of the delightful passion,
You brown haired witch, you eclipse them all,
Who aspire to such pretensions.

Lotta. Then you love me so? Monte.

Sumner. Love, love you? The word expresses not
The power 'tis said to represent; it falls short
Of my affection. When in the rushing tide
Of adversity, that might darken your path
In future years, (for most all, there is such a time,)
Remember well what now I tell you:
You are mine, and will so continue till you die.
No other in love's embrace shall clasp
This waist, or kiss those lips, but I.
This love is your first, it shall be your last.

Lotta. Little I knew the power of love before.
What is it? I cannot say. Did I possess
The eloquence of a Webster or a Clay,
I could not picture it as it is.

I do not wish to know. To attempt to explain
Would be to overstep the bounds of romance;
Then appears the cold philosophy of nature.
Reason, I do not want in love, love is sentiment
And reason and sentiment are opponents:
Two extremes that make the trials of life.
He who can combine the two, is a character,
An exception. I wish to be lost in sentiment's depths,
To only know, that I love you
And you love me; I care to know no more.

Sumner. By that unconscious philosophy, my darling,
You have declared Love's true inspiration.

Lotta. But poor Hazel and the Lieutenant; I am
afraid the path of love will be hard with them. Mama
has such strict notions of what constitutes love; the foundation is gold, that is her dogma.

Sumner. They will not have the great trouble you
imagine.

Lotta. I believe you Monte. You always speak in
such a way as though what's wanted to be done is as good
as done.

Sumner. No, love, there will be two brides, two
grooms to march to the music of Mendelssohn and
Wagner.

Lotta. Did you know Papa's will is to be read to-day?

Sumner. Is it? I should like to be present to know its
provisions; it may contain much of importance even to
myself; he intimated to me once to that effect.

Lotta. Yes, to all of us. Senator Choate will be here
at two o'clock, he was Papa's lawyer.

Sumner. Let me draw on my memory; was he not the gentleman I met the night of the reception, two months ago?

Lotta. Yes, the same person; he is one of the finest lawyers in the country; he was in the United States Senate for several terms.

Sumner. I remember now. Did he not introduce that celebrated bill to pension—*Exit with Lotta.*

Enter Lieut. and Hazel; do not see Sumner and Lotta.

Lieut. Tramps—no, no; the frontier boys are some of Nature's finest specimens of men.

Hazel. I have been thinking you had better let me speak to Mama.

Lieut. But to do that would be a poor commentary on my manliness.

Hazel. Do not consider it so. Reflect how different Mama is from most mothers; I really believe I could do more than did you address her on the subject.

Lieut. Very well, dear. You shall act as you have reasoned: the wish for your success will be the running subject of my anxiety.

Hazel. She is coming now; step into the conservatory to await the decision.—*Exit Lieut.*—My confidence of success is disturbed by dread, but it is better that I break the ice of uncertainty and suspense.

Mrs. Fremont. Alone, Hazel? I am glad you are, I wish to speak to you on an important matter. I have noticed of late, that Lieutenant Silverton has paid you great attention; have you encouraged him?

Hazel. Why Mama—Lieutenant Silverton—has been a little—in fact—I was—going to ask—if you—would——

Mrs. Fremont. Would what?

Hazel. Con—sent.

Mrs. Fremont. Is it possible it has come to this? do you inform me that he has proposed? that—that you have accepted him? he, does he flatter himself he is your chosen one? that he can marry you?

Hazel. Oh, Mama! Mama! don't——

Mrs. Fremont. Hush child! he is not for you. His attentions must cease at once. Why, what is he? who is he? Nothing but a common lieutenant; doomed to live the best portion of his life on the frontier with cowboys, or in Alaska with the Esquimaux. He is of good family and there his value ends. He is penniless. I did not intentionally introduce to my family a fortune hunter.

Hazel. But—but—Mama—I love—him.

Mrs. Fremont. Love! what is love? The cause of half the misery that holds the world in bondage. Has he been here today? I shall see him; his visits shall in future cease.

Enter Lotta.

Lotta. Oh! Mama! what would you do? What have you done?

Hazel. Sobbing.—Lotta, Lotta.

Mrs. Fremont. Stop child, stop! Let me hear no more.

Lotta. Mama, think of Hazel's happiness; she loves the Lieutenant; think of yourself when you were a girl.

Mrs. Fremont. Yes, I married for love, what resulted? poverty, neglect and misery. I married again for money, the result, all the comforts money could buy: would you have been here today, in this house dressed as you are, your every wish gratified and all that wealth can give, had I not married Jackson?

Lotta. That is your own life, others have different feelings; have a little consideration for theirs.

Mrs. Fremont. Lotta, you forget yourself; you know not what you say. I have had years of experience you are innocent of the world's ways.

Lotta. Then Mama, if that is to be Hazel's answer; give me mine; I love and am loved in return; I have accepted Mr. Sumner for my future husband.

Mrs. Fremont. I congratulate you on your choice. Mr. Sumner is a perfect gentleman, a man of business and of the world; though I know nothing of his family connections, he is wealthy.

Enter Mrs. Kelton.

Hazel. Mama, how can you be so cruel, so heartless?

Mrs. Kelton. Now Matilda, why need you be so severe? The Lieutenant has expectations.

Mrs. Fremont. Mother, stop right where you are! I have given my decision; if Hazel persists in his acquaintance, I shall cut off her inheritance.

Mrs. Kelton. Matilda! Matilda Fremont! What are you threatening? The Lieutenant is a noble man; he deeply loves Hazel and will make her happy. Hazel, continue true to the Lieutenant, you shall have my property.

Mrs. Fremont. Mother! will you stop? I shall take Hazel to Europe this very week and remain until this infatuation of hers is cured. Do not oppose me; you know my will; do you wish to add more to my troubles? We shall see!—*Starts to exit—Mrs. Kelton follows.*

Mrs. Kelton. We shall see! I am nearing my eightieth

year and yet owner of the old homestead; and Hazel and
Lotta may count themselves as heirs to every acre, every
inch.—*Exit Mrs. Kelton and Mrs. Fremont.*

Lotta. Don't cry, Hazel dear, it may all be well yet.
Ray is here, and he as the object of this trouble can add
greater comfort than I, so will leave you.—*Exit.*

Enter Lieut.

Hazel. Ah, Ray! Ray——

Lieut. I knew it, I foresaw the result. Come, come,
you will be mine yet; Monte will help me.

Hazel. What can he do?

Lieut. He will assist us in some way; I tell you he is
a friend not owned at random.

Hazel. Can't—can't we run away?

Lieut. Exactly my plan; unless something favorable
happens tomorrow, I shall steal you away in the afternoon
to a justice' court in Jersey; the justice settles many cases
of a life's pursuing sorrow.

Hazel. Hope then will be my strength; to live alone—
to live without you, I could not do. What is life without
love? What is marriage without one you love. I almost
envy Lotta; she has her consent but I am denied mine.

Lieut. Those tears, my darling, are to me
The saddest humor to the disastrous ending
Of this well-meant and reasoned attempt.
Fear not, I know there will advent brighter hours;
Let this answer rest lightly on your thoughts;
And remember, what some men may say,
Will often mark a victory in a day.
Here comes Monte.

Hazel. Then I will leave you.—*Exit.*

Enter Sumner.

Sumner. The blues again, or thinking, which? Has Mrs. Fremont rendered her decision, that you look so grave?

Lieut. Yes; it is no she said for me, and yes for you: for you I rejoice; for myself I am miserable; most damnably so.

Sumner. Then change the existing burden of the mood, take on a lighter one and become most damnably happy. Are you so weak as to allow a woman's will to overcome yours? If she were a queen and you a much be-chained and prisoned subject, you might well put the hour to fret; but on such slight occasion you have but need to exercise your courage, and at the end to exclaim I've won! I've won!

Lieut. Right! your reasoning never fails to give me a feeling of comfort; gloomy thoughts I am quite subject to: though a soldier's maxim should be, "Command yourself and you command an Empire." I fear the empire will never acknowledge the wisdom of my ways and reason, for the fact I cannot yet claim what needs me most at present.

Enter Mrs. Fremont; Lieut. steps forward; Sumner retires to one corner, unseen by stage.

Lieut. Mrs. Fremont—

Mrs. Fremont. We are on the same errand. Lieutenant Silverton, I did not imagine you would presume on the freedom of our social circle extended to you by me; to make love, propose and engage yourself to my daughter. Had I thought such would be the outcome, you would never have been admitted. Of you personally, I have naught to say against; the family which you represent is

one of age and title, and they have my greatest respect;
to you financially I have the greatest objection, which is
most vital to the happiness of my daughter; my request is
that your attentions and visits cease henceforth.

Sumner.   Aside.—"So mote it be."

Lieut.   Mrs. Fremont, to me you have extended as you
say, a courtesy in the admission of myself to the social
circle of which you are leader; but for me to speak, to
dance, to be honored with your daughter's company and
not love her, would be to charge me with a will of iron,
a stoic's heart, two qualities I do not possess; to be a
woman hater, to brand me as cold and heartless, unworthy
a true woman's love.

Mrs. Fremont.   You are entirely too susceptible and
should not run loose in society.

Sumner.   Aside.--Ray might exclaim at intervals,
'Girls beware, I'm silly.'

Lieut.   So it was my family that gave me the freedom
Of your set.   The American with a lineage
Must have it backed with coin, or he stands
Little chance with the foreigner, titled
And insolvent.   True my ancestry is influential
In its name, but here for once it's ceased
To work: yet the strength of a pedigree endures,
And forms always an interesting theme
To the untitled public of a republic;
For there are they, that regard with awe,
The noble rogues of other days.
Were my ancestors feudal slaves, you'd not
Hear the boast of heraldry valued by me
In its moldy worth and memories; but being
A patrician, born of patricians, I beg

Your thoughtful consideration of the fact;
And may its worm-eaten value never fade,
Though I fear it has.   An exponent
Of the common herd, I'll feel disgraced
To be thus viewed.   Sweet slumbering
Castled memories, abbied skeletons and
Haunted lodge's tales; do bolster up my claim
To be a descendant of a gouted race of nobles;
Which avails me not.

Permit me to say, that in my judgment the woman who
values her daughter's happiness in life by the amount of
ducates she will bring in the matrimonial market, is unworthy of the name of mother.

Mrs. Fremont.   Sir! such language——

Lieut.   That is all, Mrs. Fremont; I bid you good
afternoon.

Enter Cicero.

Cicero.   Sentah Choate am in de parlor.

Mrs. Fremont.   Show him in.—*Exit Cicero.*

Enter Choate.   Converses with Mrs. Fremont.

Sumner.   Aside to Lieut.—Remain, Ray, where you
are.

Lieut.   I can't, old boy, I can't; it's against all rules of
etiquette.

Sumner.   Don't place such value on etiquette; remain
as a favor to me.

Lieut.   Well, for you then, awhile.

Mrs. Fremont.   *Rings bell.*— You   are   prompt,
Senator.

Choate.   I value promptness; it made my success in life.

Enter Cicero.

Mrs. Fremont. Acquaint Mrs. Kelton and the young ladies that the Senator is here to read the will.—*Exit Cicero.*

Lieut. *To Sumner.* The will! I was a witness to it.

Sumner. Then it is well you remained.

Choate. Ah, Mr. Sumner, Lieutenant; glad to see you, gentlemen. It is fortunate you are here, Lieutenant, you were a witness to this will.

Lieut. Yes, I did attest to its execution.

Enter Hazel, Lotta and Mrs. Kelton. Hazel starts to go toward the Lieut.

Mrs. Fremont. Hazel, I want you with me.

Choate. Good day, ladies. Now to unfold the mysteries of this instrument.—*Opens will.*

NEW YORK, Nov. 20, 18——.
In the name of God: Amen.

I, Jackson Fremont, a resident of the City, County and State, of New York; being of sound mind and memory, do of my own free will and accord, after all just and lawful claims against my estate are paid in full, bequeath the following portions of properties, claimed by me and known as my own. To wit:

Item First: To my wife, Mrs. Jackson Fremont; one-third of the aggregate amount of all real estate, stocks, bonds, bank accounts, and various commercial interests held by me.

Mrs. Fremont.—A third!

Choate.—Item Second: The remaining two-thirds of the aggregate amount of all real estate, stocks, bonds, bank accounts and various commercial interests held by me; go free and unconditionally to Mr. Montgomery Sumner, of Tombstone, Arizona.

All surprised; Mrs. Fremont attempts to speak; Choate motions silence.

Item third: I further appoint Mr. Montgomery Sumner to be the legal executor of this will, without bonds.

In witness whereof, I hereunto set my hand and seal and decree this to be my last will and testament, in presence of these witnesses.

[SEAL.]   (Signed.) JACKSON FREMONT.

           FARNWELL CHOATE,

Witnesses: Attorney and Notary Public.

LIEUT. RAY SILVERTON, Hotel Metropole.

HORATIO WEST, No. ——, Lexington Ave.

Mrs. Fremont. What! The property left to Mr. Sumner?

Lieut. To Monte!

Mrs. Kelton. Why! Why! this is strange!

Hazel. Mr. Sumner!

Lotta. Papa and Mr. Sumner were great friends.

Sumner. Aside.—Heaven conferred on me a talent, I put to good account; in consequence fortune assails me with her gifts.

Mrs. Fremont. Senator, have you read aright? leave this property to Mr. Sumner?

Choate. Quite right, Mrs. Fremont. I confess it does slightly astonish me.

Mrs. Fremont. Impossible! How is this? Mr. Sumner, that you are made an executor of this property, and that you are a recipient of two-thirds of its value? Who are you? Tell me that, sir? You were but a stranger to my house two months ago. Senator, I say that Fremont was insane when he made that will; I protest against it; it is an outrage.

Choate. The will is valid. If ever a man was sane of mind, Fremont was, the time he wrote that will; is it not so, Lieutenant?

Lieut. It is so.

Mrs. Fremont. Yes, vindicate yourselves, conspirators!

Choate. Madam, add respectful care to you speech.

Sumner. If I may be left to a private interview with Mrs. Fremont, I can explain how Mr. Fremont came to make me an heir—

Mrs. Fremont. An heir!

Sumner. To his estate and its executor. Their existed a bond of friendship between us, stronger than the ties of husband and wife. If you will permit me, ladies and gentlemen.—*All exit.*

Choate. Aside.—I remember now, when he eulogized Fremont, he said they were great friends.—*Exit.*

Mrs. Fremont. Speak, sir! What is the meaning of this will? I never heard Mr. Fremont mention your name previous to your introduction to our house.

Sumner. Not by the name of Sumner, no; but possibly by the name of Emory.

Mrs. Fremont. Emory! Emory! What of it? you'r not Emory!

Sumner. No, were I John Emory, it would be a compliment to Nature's treatment of me that she should have kept the wrinkles from my brow, the silver from my hair for so many years. Hardly old John Emory, your first husband, but his representative by blood; I am Walter Emory your son——

Mrs. Fremont. My son! You'r not my son! he died in Sonora, Old Mexico, years ago; he and his father! You are an impostor—you are——

Sumner. Mother dear, your memory fails. Your accusations are unjust. Fifteen years make great changes, and I have changed. Mother,—*Holds out hand.*— Perhaps Mama would sound more like home; Mama dear, are you glad to see your boy?

Mrs. Fremont. Keep away from me! This is outrageous! this—even were you my son, I care nothing for you; you are nought to me but a stranger: I shall not recognize you.

Sumner. Aside.—The chilling atmosphere of my
    companion's company
Makes merry with my sensitive feelings.
My mother does not recognize me
With maternal kiss and warm embrace;
I'm quite at a loss of what to do;
Shall I weep? And yet the world
Will wonder why some men are cruel.

Mrs. Fremont. I repeat, sir; how came this property left to you? Your claiming to be Walter Emory, answers not the question. I shall contest this will to the bitter end, not a dollar, not a cent, shall you receive.

Sumner. That's for the judge to say.
Do you realize that you cast shame
On the sacred title of mother?
You as that, are at level with the uncivilized;
Uncharitable as the Hindoo that casts
Her child to the crocodiles of the Ganges;
She's impelled by religious motives,
Your religion is Mammon worship.

The Hindoo has more motherly love than makes up
That passion of your soul. Of course
In point of education there is a difference.
This is a home coming:
The prodigal and I, meet in extremes.

Mrs. Fremont. How came this will so? Why are
you mentioned in it?

Sumner. Fremont was the direct cause of my sorrows:
He robbed my father of me, and a paying claim;
He robbed me of my father, and an inheritance.
But for him I'd be a collegiate; instead
The great, bitter, cold, heartless world,
Did my education with experience as master.
No regrets for that; 'twas a good thing 'twas so.
Our bitterest woes are often our greatest blessings.
I have found home at last—O, what a home—
Not such a home as Paine immortalized in song.
Had I tears, and I probably have; I might
Shed them: did I rub my eyes with an onion.
But to reply, Mrs. Fremont, Mama;
I know not how it was, he must have repented
On receiving the history of my life: I wrote
Over a year ago, when in hard straits and
Asked a partial consideration.
The pity of his heart has spoken;
Though I unanswered then, am answered now;
A surprise as strange to me, as is to you.
It was a crime of the soul, not of the hand:
This will does tardy honor to his memory.

*Bowie is here being shown in; on seeing scene raises
his hand and stops the announcement of his presence by*

Cicero, who exits. Bowie seats himself to one side, unobserved by stage.

Mrs. Fremont. You'r no more to me, what once you were;

An intriguer now, then you were a child.

By emotional eloquence, of fact or fancy,

You have stolen what should be mine.

Two thirds! why stop at two?

He should have left you three.

Where are your proofs,

To make known to the law your right?

For by another week you can testify

To the probate judge this romantic story,

Of how you hoodwinked an insane man.

Sumner. I have but one proof, a gentleman that I appointed with to be here at this hour, but he has not arrived.

Bowie. He is here.

Mrs. Fremont. Turns quickly, shrieks.—John!— *Sinks on sofa, showing great nervousness.*

Sumner. You do honor to the virtue of promptness. Allow me, Mrs. Fremont, to make you on conversational terms with Mr. Bowie from Chihuahua.

Bowie. Yes, Mrs. Fremont, fifteen years has been an epoch in our lives; but considering your memory for our son is deficient, it holds good for me. You readily believed Fremont's tale of our deaths, and received a fortune in exchange for that belief; the gold I struggled for on the sagebrush plains and mountains of Nevada and Arizona, ultimately to find in the Sierra Madras. My partner conceived the brilliant idea of my starving in the mountains as compensation for my pains. Some waits in this life, at times are long, very long; but the wait is as a dog's tail, it has an end. Yet all can't reckon up; it is the boy's and my triumph now; that portion of the property of Fremont's formerly mine, falls to our son, Walter Emory, otherwise Mr. Sumner from Tombstone. Mr. Bowie and his son, Mr. Sumner, will undertake to enjoy life; an occupation they have never followed; but will attempt to quickly learn the duties of its following.— *Takes Sumner's arm and starts to go, walks to center door.*

Sumner. Aside to Bowie.—Leave the house quickly. I will meet you at the Hoffman, five sharp.

Bowie. At five.—*Exit.*

Sumner. To those without.—Your attendance now, ladies and gentlemen.—*Enter all.*—Senator, explanations have been in order and Mrs. Fremont understands.

Choate. I am happy to learn all points have been amicably settled; it would hardly be in keeping with the house of Fremont, to have a legal squabble over the will.

Mrs. Kelton. Matilda, you don't look well.

Mrs. Fremont. I—I—*Hand to heart.*—My digital——

Mrs. Kelton. Hazel, the medicine! Oh! Help! She is dying!—She is dead.

Hazel. O, Mama, speak! only speak to Hazel.

Lotta. Just a word, Mama; only speak.

Choate. This is frightful, but may be she has only fainted.

Lieut. Rings bell.—Enter Cicero.

Lieut. A doctor, call a doctor quick!—*Exit Cicero.*

Sumner. Aside.—An exit well accomplished.

Lieut. Heart failure.

Mrs. Kelton. At last; it's come at last; poor Matilda; I knew she would never stand another shock.

Sumner. *Aside.*—Till future cause for change arrives,
My father's name shall remain Mr. Bowie;
I shall continue the alias my death.
This family history must keep hidden
Underneath the monument, inscribed,
'To all that is mortal of old memories.'
Therein sheltered from the world's inquiring gaze,
Will be entombed the misty legend, the tradition,
Known to me alone; another added mystery
To the ancient Azetc Mine of Chihuahua.

FINIS.

EPILOGUE.

Sumner.

Why need there be an epilogue
To this peculiar case?
Whereas in Shakespeare's time the tendency
Was to write life as it should be;
In this pedantic and interrogatory age
We essay to write as existence is.
A limited comprehension would not ask
Who's the villain, but say I:
'For if he's not a villain, what's the designation?
Some will oppose the assertion.
I am good, generous at times; in the
Countless ways, that generosity and forbearance
Is loved to be received by him or her or brute:
Many stand to swear the fact with voice or look,
If ingratitude has not dulled their love of me.
Many will say I turn out too well;
I might use the finale pistol, possibly
Mesmerise myself to a never awakening
Trance-like state, undying and yet dead.
Rascals usually die in the last act;
I don't consider this the last act, or I a rogue.
How many sympathize with me? a great many;
How many dare tell others of this sympathy?
A very few.